Speaking
for
Ourselves

Speaking for Ourselves

SHORT STORIES BY JEWISH LESBIANS

edited by
Irene Zahava

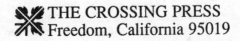 THE CROSSING PRESS
Freedom, California 95019

Grateful acknowledgment is given to the following authors, for permission to include previously published work:

Jyl Lynn Felman: "Crisis," from *Sinister Wisdom 27.*
Judy Freespirit: "The Trouble with Theaters," from *Common Lives/Lesbian Lives 21.*
Ellen Gruber Garvey: "Bubbe Meiseh (Grandmother's Tale)," from *Sinister Wisdom 31* and "Soup Story," from *The Minnesota Review,* Fall 1987.
Jano: "The Woman Who Lied," from *Common Lives/Lesbian Lives 29.*
Melanie Kaye/Kantrowitz: "My Jewish Face," from *Response* and *Sinister Wisdom 35.* Also from a forthcoming collection of the author's short stories, to be published by Spinsters/ Aunt Lute in 1990.
Lesléa Newman: "Right Off the Bat," from a forthcoming collection of the author's short stories, *Secrets,* to be published by New Victoria Publishers in 1990.
Thyme S. Siegel: "My Mother Was a Light Housekeeper," from *The Woman Who Lost Her Names: Selected Writings by American Jewish Women,* compiled and edited by Julia Wolf Mazow (Harper & Row, 1980).
Judith Stein: "The Thirteenth Passenger," from *Common Lives/Lesbian Lives 18.*

Cover illustration and design by Betsy Bayley
Book design and production by Martha Waters

Printed in the U.S.A.

Library of Congress Cataloging-in-Publication Data

Speaking for ourselves : short stories by Jewish lesbians / edited by
  Irene Zahava.
    p.   cm.
  ISBN 0-89594-429-4   ISBN 0-89594-428-6 (pbk.)
  1. Lesbians—Fiction. 2. Women, Jewish—Fiction. 3. Lesbians'
writings, American. 4. Short stories, American—Women authors.
5. Short stories, American—Jewish authors. I. Zahava, Irene.
PS648.L47S64 1990
813'.01089287—dc20
                                    89-77903
                                    CIP

Contents

Preface

When I was in the sixth grade I dreamed that my classmates and I were herded into a large gymnasium and told to sit in a circle. Nikita Kruschev and John Kennedy walked among us, looking us over. Kruschev stopped in front of me, noticed that I was wearing a Jewish star around my neck, bent over and yanked the star from its chain. He put it in his pocket and walked off. Kennedy followed him, never saying a word. I woke up feeling terrified.

When I was twenty years old and a junior in college I moved into my boyfriend's apartment. One night I dreamed that I was sleeping next to a woman. While I dreamed, I reached my hand out and began to caress my boyfriend's body, imagining that it was a woman's body. When my hand finally touched his face, and I felt his long beard and scratchy mustache beneath my fingers, I was so startled that I woke up . . . disappointed and frustrated, but with the clear knowledge that this relationship was over, and my life was about to move in a new direction.

I've thought about these two dreams as I've worked on this anthology and I've thought about what it means to be both a Jew and a lesbian in our society. It's not easy to be singled out as being different, to hear the words kike and dyke spoken with disdain and contempt. At the same time, I know that there are ways in which I choose to be different, and that I delight in those things which set me apart. I try to embrace these contradictions and to accept the presence of loose threads and untidy corners in my life.

The women who have contributed stories to this collection also grapple with contradictions and conflicts. Their experiences are not identical; they don't all come from the same place, share the same visions or speak with the same voice. Each woman speaks for herself, and by doing so she adds to the growing body of work that describes and explores the reality of what it means to be a Jewish lesbian.

Irene Zahava
January, 1990

My Jewish Face

MELANIE KAYE/KANTROWITZ

IT WAS THE EXACT BLEND of rage and fun that got me hooked on politics in the first place: deciding something had to be done and forming a group and doing it — immediately. Like Abbie Hoffman and Jerry Rubin — Jews and Yippies — used to say, *Do it!*, and if Jerry Rubin ended up on Wall Street (a source of some humiliation to those of us who measure Jewish safety by constantly counting which side which Jews are on), Abbie Hoffman, as it turned out, had been plugging along underground all those years with his new name and plastic surgery new Jewish face: still doing it.

    We did it too — in this case, interrupted a performance we found insulting and made the audience to some extent ours; a modest but nonetheless thrilling feat. What I remember most vividly, though, is not what we did or even how I felt. It's Rae I remember and it's her face I can see right this minute up on stage in front of the cafe as the theater company was singing their stupid finale. Because she was part of the company, one of "them," and when it came to her part, she betrayed them and announced herself.

1

The story doesn't start that night in the cafe. For me, for the rest of the group, it starts in the afternoon around the lunch table. For Fran and Bonnie it started the night before, when they had gone to the cafe to see political theater. But for Rae it started when she was an infant: orphaned, adopted, raised in a churchgoing family. At 17 she discovered that her grandmother was alive and a Jew, a survivor from Hungary. Rae had hitchhiked across the country to spend what turned out to be the last six months of the old woman's life with her. Then she hitchhiked back, came out as a lesbian, and hovered uneasily around her Jewishness like it was a gorgeous book in a foreign language. She didn't know it but she craved it. She was 19, tall and large-boned with high Slavic cheeks, grey eyes, dark nearly straight hair. She joined the theater company.

It was her second show with them, early rehearsal. In one skit was a joke about the Holocaust, scraping the bottom of the bad taste barrel, and you're probably wondering about the joke; maybe afraid you'd find it funny. I wouldn't repeat it even if I remembered it, but it wasn't funny. In the same skit was a crack about animals looking Jewish. Each unfunny joke reinforced the other and Rae felt queasy. She said so.

The director of the theater company, a nubile man-loving sort of woman named Janet, ridiculed her. No one in the company stood up for Rae, predictably not even the one other Jew, who instead spoke the line that should be engraved next to (the by now somewhat hackneyed) *when they came for the x's I said nothing because I wasn't an x until finally they came for me.* The line I'm talking about is, *I'm Jewish and I don't think it's anti-Semitic.* So much for solidarity. Rae was 19 and had been a conscious Jew for two years. She'd had no Jewish education, no exposure to Jewish culture or tradition, until the six months with her grandmother. In this she was not so different from a lot of American Jews, except for the six months part. She backed down and shut up.

2

And stayed shut up until that night on the stage.

But first comes afternoon, and at the lunch table Fran was upset. *It was disgusting*, she gestured with her coffee cup, luckily almost empty. *There was a joke about the Holocaust and there was a woman wiggling around barking and meowing. The last line of the scene is, "She looks Jewish, doesn't she?" About the dog-cat character, whichever it was.* Fran waved her cup again, this time in dismissal.

Bonnie had taken off her glasses and was rubbing between her eyebrows. *The whole time I was saying to myself, "Is this happening, am I being crazy?"*

Where was this? Shelly was asking, *a play, what kind of play?* And Zelda, *Who are these people?*

We were sitting in the cafeteria of a large Midwestern college campus. Thousands of women had gathered for a feminist conference, a small group of us had coalesced just two days before in the Jewish caucus. Women had come from the South, from the West Coast, from the East, some it's true because they were teachers and their schools were paying, but some because they were dying for contact with other Jewish feminists and lesbians. We came to feed our Jewish selves: those already wrapped in scraps of knowledge, history, culture, religion, who came to piece together something more whole, and the rest of us, like me, who had only our Jewish names, faces, scattered memories, and hunger for more. We were delighted with each other, gathering every day for lunch — we figured people would say we were clannish no matter what so we might as well enjoy ourselves. One day Zelda and Penny did Midrash about Ruth and Naomi, for Shavuos, and I had never even known their story was connected to Shavuos, nor that Ruth was a convert to Judaism and the mother of King David. As a lesbian with a gentile lover, I was moved by Ruth's devotion, a woman to another woman, and by the idea that someone could join a people through love. Zelda, on the other hand, hated the story, found the women weak and shadowy, cherished only for the sons they bore; she had been married for 20 years and kept an orthodox home, this Zelda, and she preferred the story of Judith, who chopped off Holofernes' head. *Never pigeonhole anyone,* I reminded myself not for the last time.

Another day we learned songs, Yiddish from Shelly, Hebrew from Fran, and we sang more and more vigorously until we were grabbing each other's hands for a jumping kicking line dance around the cafeteria, several minutes worth before the polite but appalled manager asked us to stop. Still another day we talked about the Middle East, the Israeli peace movement, icy tension clamping down on everyone's temples and shoulders as our feared differences emerged. And there were differences. But still we were talking.

Today it had turned into a meeting. The night before Fran and Bonnie had gone into town to the local hip cafe where a political theater group was performing the series of skits. After two days of delicious Jewish pride, one skit's throwaway insensitivity and contempt had so stunned them that they had sat there quietly incredulous. They hadn't even thought of telling anyone. But over lunch, when Zelda asked Bonnie in all innocence what she'd done last night, Bonnie started talking, and then everyone was tossing questions on the table.

This is supposed to be radical theater, like the Mime Troupe or something?

Did anyone else seem upset?

What do you think they were doing?

What did they *think they were doing?*

Did you talk to the actors?

We went this morning, Fran said, *to talk to someone, a couple of them were there —*

Yeah, they spared us 3.67 minutes — Bonnie interjected.

We spoke with the woman who directed it, Janet—she wrote the script, she played the cat/dog creature—

Bonnie: *— watching her fawn and wriggle was bad enough, she's just a bundle of talent —*

What is this, Animal Farm?, Sonia stuck in.

Fran went on: *Janet didn't know Nazi propaganda described Jews as dogs. She thanked us for telling her, but of course she didn't mean anything by it. The joke about the Holocaust wasn't supposed to make fun of the Holocaust. That isn't what she meant.* Bonnie made a tight prissy face and we all laughed.

What she meant was — sort of va-ague — Bonnie's voice went up and down *— but something like we were all Nazis —*

I can't stand that liberal bullshit — Shelly shook her head in disgust *— "If I'm Not OK, You're Not OK Either?"*

No, Sonia interrupted, *it's an old game people play— "We're All Nazis," you never heard of it?*

Also known as — I broke into song, the tune "Clementine" *— "If Everyone's Guilty, No One's Responsible,"* linking my arm through Sonia's, but Fran began again —

She kept insisting she hadn't meant anything —

—so we shouldn't feel anything, Bonnie snorted. *Then she had to go. She certainly wasn't about to change anything just because we were upset. She kept talking about artistic freedom — and we understood, she was SO busy —*

She thought we were crazy. Fran looked depressed and I wondered if she'd been called crazy a lot.

Oversensitive, Bonnie corrected, making her funny little prissy face again, and we all laughed on cue.

The cafeteria was nearly empty, the time allotted for lunch was over and I could feel a restless energy perched in the middle of the table. I have been an organizer on and off for more than half my adult life — civil rights, women's libera-

5

tion; since I got hooked, like I said. I recognized that energy. It was people wanting to fight back but uncertain what to do. I know when people want to fight and do nothing, what gets reinforced is feeling helpless, like you can't fight city hall, can't stick up for your friends or your people or your self, can't do anything. Everyone's sense of possibility shrinks up a little. To me, that restless energy is the sheerest temptation, whereas blocking that energy — out of fear, laziness or just plain lack of imagination — is my idea of sin.

What do you want to do? I asked. The word *do* hung in the air, an odd moment of quiet.

Carla broke it. *We could go to the play and start a discussion when it's over.*

Tame, distinctly tame. Zelda wrinkled her nose.

We could just interrupt the performance — we could give out leaflets. Shelly was getting excited.

We can't get a leaflet together by tonight, I responded automatically and immediately felt ashamed: Why was I offhandedly dismissing the idea? Who knew what we could do?

Let's picket — Zelda was piling her tray high with everyone's dishes — *I have to go do my workshop now. Someone let me know what's happening, I'm up for whatever, OK?*

Me too. I have to drop off Lila. Lila was Sonia's year-old baby, on a breastfeeding break from childcare. *What about guerilla theater, right at the entrance, we could do our own play.* I resisted the impulse to say we couldn't get a play together so quickly.

Can you get childcare for tonight? Penny was asking.

Yeah, we'll all chip in, Zelda tossed off over her shoulder.

But Bonnie and Fran were beginning to feel contortions of self-doubt.

What if we just took it wrong?

I can't remember exactly what gets said, what if we're being —

— *paranoid?* I asked, and we all laughed, rather bitterly.

When are we sure, Shelly asked acidly, *when they're marching us to the showers? Or do we say, "Well, maybe we need to wash."*

But they were adamant. The responsibility was too heavy. They wanted the rest of us to see the play so we could act on our knowledge, not their feelings. We would attend the performance, paying for tickets — which annoyed the shit out of Shelly and me but that's what people wanted to do — and, when (or if?) offensive things got said, we would simply say what we thought, force them to deal with our reactions.

So there we were, $6 a head. I have to say the show was unbelievably unfocused and just plain vapid. There was a skit about unemployment, a couple about TV and advertising — really bold subjects; one about American racism — unintentionally but distinctly racist; one about the Statue of Liberty, in which poor Rae was the Statue, except we didn't know Rae yet, she was just a large young woman, one of the actors: them. Half the jokes revolved around parts of her body. The overall message thrummed home with the subtlety of a buffalo herd was, *it's your own fault if you don't do anything* (definitely a variation on the *we're all Nazis* theme).

So we sat in the audience waiting to be or not to be offended enough to do something: It. There was Janet scooting around barking and meowing and wiggling her small prized ass. There was the not funny joke about the Holocaust, and I said to myself in an affectionate but bossy tone, *OK, honey, you encouraged everyone else, you go first* and I was on my feet asking in a very loud voice: *You think that's funny?*

Shelly said later when she saw me start to get up and

7

heard the words come out of my mouth her heart began to pound so fast she thought she'd have a heart attack. *It's really happening,* she thought, *now we have to go through with it.*

One after the other, we did. Shelly spoke next, with a slow measured anger that was itself an irresistible force — *I have to say this very clearly, and I want everyone to understand it. The Holocaust is not funny. There is nothing funny about it.* Dead silence while people combed the Holocaust for something funny. You could see them not coming up with anything.

Do you know who's in your audience? Sonia was asking, *Maybe people who lost their families, or people who were tortured. You're supposed to be against torture.*

We are against torture, oh, of course, Janet the cat/dog nodded emphatically.

But your jokes add to people's pain, people who've suffered what no one should ever suffer. Why? Why would you want to make jokes about this? Penny was asking with an inexplicable touching innocence. *People were — killed, tortured. By Nazis, or even now it's happening in Salvador, right now — you make it trivial, what they go through. Laughable. I know that's not what you want,* she concluded sweetly.

I'm not sure they don't want that, Shelly quipped under her breath, but I was crying. I was sure the audience felt it too, a gap outlined in neon between the cheap shallow politics of the skits and the depth of these women.

Zelda was talking now. *Why are you saying a dog looks Jewish? Do you know Nazi propaganda said Jews were dogs? Do you know people, Jews, Gypsies, homosexuals, communists were treated like animals, worse than animals?* and Bonnie, *You're supposed to be against oppression. We're saying this skit is oppressive.*

Janet, deprived of some dignity by her tail and whiskers, kept saying, *You don't understand what we're trying to do, let us finish* — and one of the men who'd played too convincingly a creep pawing the Statue of Liberty whines, *We're on your side.* Several of the actors looked stricken, as if they couldn't quite believe our ingratitude.

It doesn't matter what you're trying to do — I put a hard edge on the word "trying" — *what matters is what you're doing. We're telling you it's not working.*

The whole point of political theater is that people shouldn't be passive, Carla was waving her arms, *why do you expect us to sit quiet and listen?* You could feel at least half the audience mentally nodding, *Really!*

So the actors insisted on their intentions, we counterinsisted that intentions — in art as in life — were the least of it, and finally we agreed to let them finish the show in return for an open discussion with the audience as soon as the play ended. Which did not stop us — by now, imagine the adrenalin — from commenting loudly on anything that bugged us as the play proceeded.

Who remembers the rest of the skits? I was just waiting for the show to end so we could have the discussion. At last came the finale. The cast gathered on stage at the front of the cafe to sing, each actor in turn, a verse about her or his character from the last skit. Each verse ended with the line, *see how you like my face,* sung 3 times, more or less musically. It was the turn of the large young woman who'd played the Statue of Liberty, she sang her verse like everyone else, concluding with *see how you like my face, see how you like my face* — she tossed her head slightly, the words came through clenched teeth — *see how you like my Jewish-looking face.*

She was crying, that was why she had clenched her teeth. You could see a wave blip through the other actors like they hadn't expected it, and sure enough Bonnie was whispering into my right ear, *That didn't happen last night.* The next actor took his turn on the song, the whole cast onstage together, and the large young woman walked right off the stage behind the screen they all entered and exited from. After a few minutes she came back out and sat down with us in the audience, next to Zelda who immediately took her hand and held on tight.

The play was over. There was weak scattered clapping. Then everyone started to talk. The cast charged us with censorship and with being deficient in our sense(s) of humor. We made all our points again, several times, and some new ones too, including Carla asking the company's one Black member how could she stand the show's racism (as if assuming that none of the other actors ought to mind a little racism here and there).

I watched the audience, mostly students from the college town, quiet young women, blabbing young men; a few women from the conference. The men were citing Marx and Brecht but in sterile phrases betraying their thin experience and a fatal snobbery — college radicals whose underlying theme seemed to be not "We're All Nazis" but "Ordinary Working People Are Stupid." Their language, their faces conjured up late-60s Berkeley in such thick nauseating waves that I could only wish for my dead father's ghost to bellow disgusted judgment: *theory-schmeory*, he'd say, in a construction I only two years ago learned was Yiddish-derived. The same time Rae learned about her grandmother.

Maybe some people were thinking about the issues. The discussion was lively enough, going on and on until the cafe janitor showed up to clean and lock, and people moved out to the sidewalk, still talking, arguing, waving their hands around.

The next day over lunch we rehashed the details. We wondered about the young woman whose name we had learned was Rae. Shelly and Zelda were ecstatic, making lists of possible targets, and Sonia too wanted to do *it* again and again. Carla kept insisting she had done nothing wrong by making the one Black responsible for the whole company's racism — that's not how she put it, naturally — and we argued.

Fran brought up what everyone had noticed, that she had not said a single word during the performance; she also confessed that when we interrupted the play, she was mortified and hoped people wouldn't know she was with us. She said this with an edge of self-mockery, but the other edge was real discomfort — *we had gone too far* — and I remembered what sometimes happens: People pushed beyond themselves snap shut, a reflex of fear, resentment and guilt. After that they stop meeting your eyes and avoid you altogether.

Carla's defensiveness and Fran's alienation struck two sour notes, as if to remind us change comes hard. But everyone else was hooked on *doing it:* not a bad habit, as habits go.

Word got around the conference. All day women were asking questions and, better yet, spreading fascinating rumors of women barring the exits from the theater (the size of the cafe and numbers of people grew sharply in these accounts), or forcing the entire audience into instant consciousness-raising groups on Jewish issues. Someone had heard it was all about Zionism and the PLO. A young graduate student who'd been there told each of us at least twice she had never seen anything like it, members of an audience taking power from the stage. She was pink with inspiration.

That night was the final event of the conference, a dance, and sometime towards midnight — I was punchy with fatigue — I saw Rae heading our way across the huge ballroom. She'd come to see us, and we gathered around her in a corner of the ballroom, and then around a table in the coffee shop, while she talked. For hours. That's when we found out about her childhood, her grandmother, her shame about knowing nothing Jewish.

You think you're the only one? Shelly asked.

Everything Jewish I know I learned in the last few years, Bonnie stuck in, and I, my cheeks surprisingly hot, nodded. I could tell this made Rae feel better.

Finally someone thought to ask what had happened with the theater company. Janet the director had been in a rage, especially at Rae, but also at two women who tried to defend her. After nearly twelve hours convulsed with fights, Rae had screamed *YOU may be a Nazi, I'm a JEW and I QUIT.* (At this point we all cheered.) Then she had gotten a ride over to the dance and here she was. She wasn't sure what she'd do next, for work or anything, but she was glad, she kept telling us that, we shouldn't worry we had made it hard for her, she was glad.

By now we were all crying and hugging her and each other. Then her ride showed up and we had to say goodbye, and we dug through our bags for books, polaroid snapshots, our addresses, Jewish strength we wanted to wrap her with, though the truth is she had all she needed and more. *Don't worry,* she said again, *I'll be fine.*

I *was* worrying, that's the down side of doing it, you make trouble and people get swept up into it and then you leave and they're stuck with trouble. Rae was out of a job, she had no Jewish family or community.

But I looked at her face. She had herself. She had been brave, and courage is a *mitzvah,* for her and for us, then and now as I remember Rae standing on stage, 19 years old, those large bones, grey eyes, straight hair. I doubt she often got spotted as a Jew, and it seems she chose her Jewishness. When she was 17 and found her grandmother. When she was 19, on the cafe stage. Maybe she's still choosing, in different ways, her proud angry Jewish face. Maybe I am too and that's why I remember.

Right Off
The Bat

LESLÉA NEWMAN

MY MOTHER'S A LESBIAN. That's the first thing I want you to know about me. I know it's not really about me, but it sort of is, and anyway I like people to know right off the bat so they don't get weird on me later when they find out. Like Brenda for instance. Brenda used to be my best friend, at my old school and then one day she just stopped talking to me. For no reason. I mean we didn't have a fight or anything, like the time she told Richard Culpepper I liked him, which was a lie. We didn't speak for almost a whole week that time. But this time there was no reason. I mean she crossed the hallway when she saw me coming and everything. I finally cornered her in the bathroom between homeroom and first period and asked her what was wrong. She said go away, my mom says I can't talk to you anymore. Your mother's a dyke.

Dyke is a bad word for lesbian, like Yid is a bad word for Jew. I'm Jewish too, which is another thing that makes me different. Being Jewish means I go to temple instead of church, only we hardly ever go anyway and we have Chanukah and Passover instead of Christmas and Easter. Being a lesbian means my mom loves women instead of men. Not everyone knows these words. Sometimes my mom says dyke when she's talking to her friends on the phone or something, but she says that's okay, lesbians can say dyke but straight people can't. I don't really understand that. I don't understand a lot of what my mom says or does. She's not like anyone else's mother I've ever met.

Like even what we eat. My mom won't let me eat school lunches, though sometimes I save up my allowance and buy one and throw out the lunch she's packed for me. At my old school I liked macaroni and cheese the best with chocolate pudding for dessert. My mom's not the world's greatest cook and we always fight because she wants me to eat weird stuff like tofu, which is this white square that looks like soap and tastes like nothing. Just to get her to make me a swiss cheese sandwich is a big deal, because she always has to give me a lecture about dairy products and how they clog you all up. If I'm lucky Linda will be around and tell my mom just to lay off. I like Linda. Linda's the reason we moved here in the first place, so my mom and Linda could be together. Linda's like, well, she's part of the family. She's my mother's, well, they use the word lover, but it's not like she's Casanova or anything. Lots of kids have single parents and lots of kids' moms have boyfriends. My mom has a girlfriend.

We have two bedrooms in our new house. My mom and Linda have one and I have the other. When we moved here my mom said I could paint my room any color I wanted. I said pink. She said any color except pink, but Linda said that wasn't fair and anyway I'd grow out of it sooner or later. We have a kitchen and a living room and a big yard, and a cat named Pat-the-cat. Pat-the-cat sleeps with me and Linda sleeps with my mom.

Linda found us the house and then we moved here. I like it better than my old house. My old house was really an apartment and I didn't have a room. My mom had her room and I had half the living room and my clothes were in the hall closet. I slept on a futon that we folded into a couch during the day. A futon is a weird kind of mattress my mom says is good for your back. Anyway I like the new house better — it's bigger and I have my own room, but I kind of liked it when it was just me and my mom. Except Linda was there most every weekend anyway and once in a while we'd go to her house but I didn't like that so much. I couldn't see any of my friends and even though I packed things to do like books to read or records to listen to, it always worked out that what I really felt like doing was at home. I mean how should I know on Friday afternoon when I'm packing up my stuff, that on Sunday morning I'd be just dying to hear my new Whitney Houston album? My mom would just tell me to stop kvetching — that's a Jewish word for complaining — but I never dragged her off to spend a weekend with one of my friends. Then she'd see what it was like.

Anyway, now we all live together and I know your next question — you don't even have to ask it — where's my father, right? Well this will probably shock you, but I don't have a father. I have a donor. A donor is a man who gives sperm to a sperm bank so a woman can have a baby. Oh I know all about the birds and the bees. My mom told me.

You see twelve years ago, no make that twelve years and nine months ago, my mom decided that she wanted to have a baby. And she's been a lesbian for a long time, so she certainly wasn't going to do it the old fashioned way. That's what she calls it, you know how they do it in the movies and stuff. So she used alternative insemination. She's into all kinds of alternative stuff — that's what people call her lifestyle — but that makes her kind of mad. How come straight people have a life and gay people have a lifestyle, she asked Linda once and Linda said, I don't know, maybe because gay people have hair and straight people have hairstyles? My mother thought that was hysterically funny. Personally I didn't get it at all, but she and Linda giggled for a good fifteen minutes over that one, until I rolled my eyes and said "children!" which made them laugh even more. I swear they can be so immature sometimes, much worse than me and my friends.

Anyway, what I was going to say was some people call it artificial insemination but my mom gets really mad at that. She gets mad pretty easy. She says it's not artificial, it's alternative. And there's nothing artificial about me. The way it works, see, is my mom got the sperm from the sperm bank and put it into a turkey baster and when her egg popped out, she popped the sperm in, and the rest as they say, is history.

Only my mom would say herstory. She's always changing words around so they're not sexist but I forget sometimes. Anyway, I don't think it's all that important, but my mom gets mad when I say that. Like I told you, practically everything makes her mad. Like the fact that I want to wear make-up for example. I'm not really ugly or anything, but I'm not exactly Whitney Houston either. It's bad enough being different in all the ways I've already told you about. It would really help to at least be able to look halfway normal. So just a little eye make-up and some blush, I asked her. I don't want to look loose or anything.

But my mom as usual had a fit, and went on and on about women's oppression, one of her favorite topics. She ranted and raved about how women are supposed to look a certain way and if we spent half the energy we spend on our bodies on our brains we could probably overthrow patriarchy, whatever that is, and really change the world.

Well you know by that time I was sorry I asked. It would have been a lot easier to just buy the stuff, put it on in the girls' room at school and wash it off before my mom got home from work. But Linda was great. She's the only one who knows how to calm my mother down in these situations. But Darlin', she said — that's what she calls my mom — Darlin', you're just laying your own trip on her, the same way your mother laid her own trip on you. Leave her be. She's got to make her own decisions about things. And besides, you wouldn't look so bad in a little lipstick yourself.

Yeah, I said, and anyway you're always saying how oppression is not having any choices so if you don't let me wear make-up, you're oppressing me. I knew my mother wouldn't be able to argue with that one, and I felt pretty proud of myself for thinking of it, but she just shook her head and said that was different and I didn't understand. Anyway, it doesn't really matter because she finally gave in and Linda even showed me how to put eyeliner on straight.

My mom doesn't know about things like that. She never wears dresses or anything, but Linda does. Just on special occasions. Like last year they got all dressed up to celebrate their anniversary, at a big fancy restaurant. I wanted to go too, but my mom said it was their special night, just for the two of them. She promised to bring me a surprise home from the restaurant if I wanted. I asked for something chocolate. Anyway, Linda got all dressed up in this royal blue dress with a big black belt around the waist. She even put her hair up on top of her head and wore these really cool silver earrings that have three interlocking loops and a ball in the middle. They kind of reminded me of an atom with a nucleus and protons and electrons orbiting around. Anyway, she looked really gorgeous.

My mom on the other hand, well she's not exactly the world's greatest dresser. All she ever wears are jeans and flannel shirts. And not designer jeans either — nerdy jeans from Bradlees. And in the summer she wears T-shirts with sayings on them like I AM A WOMAN. I CAN BLEED FOR DAYS AND NOT DIE. That's a white T-shirt she has with red splotches on it that stand for blood I guess. It's gross. Anyway, you get the picture. I mean her wardrobe is really pathetic. So that night she wore a pair of black jeans, a white jacket, a red shirt and a white tie. You probably think that's really weird, a woman wearing a tie, but lots of my mom's friends do. I'm kind of used to it I guess. Anyway, I can't imagine my mother in a dress. First of all she has these really hairy legs she refuses to shave, and second of all, what would she wear on her feet? She only has work boots, sneakers, and green flip flops for the summer.

So Linda and my mother got all dressed up that night. I took their picture and then off they went to have a good time. Only they didn't. Here's what happened: I guess they were in the restaurant eating their dinner and everything, and some punks figured out they were lesbians. They were probably doing something dumb, like holding hands. Anyway, while they were eating, I guess the punks scoped out which car was theirs, which wouldn't be too hard to do, since my mother has all these bumper stickers that say things like I LOVE WOMYN'S MUSIC, and YOU CAN'T BEAT A WOMAN, and one with purple letters which just says WE ARE EVERY-WHERE. It's kind of embarrassing when she takes me some-place, but I don't know if I'm more embarrassed by the bumper stickers or by the car. It's not even a car really, it's a truck, a beat up old pick-up because we aren't exactly rich or anything. So I bet my mother's old pick-up with all her bumper stickers stuck out like a sore thumb in the parking lot of that fancy restaurant with all the Mercedes Benz and Cadillacs, and whatever other kinds of cars rich people drive.

Well by the time these punks, or whoever it was, got done, my mom's truck had four slashed tires. My mom was so mad she wanted to kill somebody. Linda just got really sad and started to cry. That's what always happens — my mom gets mad and Linda gets sad. I get both, but this time I got mad, just like my mom. I mean, it was their special night and they weren't hurting anybody or anything, they were just going out to have a good time. But then something happened inside of me, and I got really angry at my mother. I mean if she would just shave her legs or put on a dress or quit holding Linda's hand on the street or something, these things wouldn't always be happening to her.

Me and my big mouth. As soon as I said it, I knew I shouldn't of. My mom tells me it's important to say how you feel, and then when I do, she always gets made at me. Haven't I taught you anything, she yelled. Then she started pacing up and down the living room delivering one of her famous speeches about oppression and blaming the victim. And then all of a sudden she just stopped. Maybe she saw I wasn't really listening because she came over to the couch and sat down next to me and held my hand.

Roo, she said, and I knew she couldn't be too mad if she was calling me Roo — that's my nickname from Winnie the Pooh. See, when I was a baby, my mom carried me around in a Snuggly and she felt like Kanga with her baby Roo. My real name's Rhonda, after my grandma Rebecca, and my nickname's Ronnie. Anyway, my mom said, Listen Roo, I know it's hard for you to understand why I live my life the way I do. You think if I just put on a skirt and shaved my legs everything would be okay. Well, your Great Aunt Zelda and your Uncle Hymie thought the exact same thing with their fancy Christmas tree on their front lawn, and still their neighbors in Poland turned them in to the Nazis for a buck fifty a piece. Remember Brenda, Ronnie? You don't need friends like that. Listen Roo, she said again, if I only teach you one thing in your whole life, it's be yourself. Be straight, be gay, be a drag queen in heels, or a bulldyke like your old ma, but be whoever you are and be proud of it, okay? Life's too short to pretend you're someone you're not, and then spend all your time worrying about what's going to happen if you get caught. I spent too many years in the closet, and no tire-slashing assholes are going to push me back. She made a fist and smacked it into her hand, hard. But she didn't hurt herself or anything. My mom studies karate, which is another weird thing she does. I watched her in her class once, where we used to live. It was pretty cool to see her punching and kicking and everything. My mom's small, and kinda skinny, but she's a lot stronger than she looks. Her teacher was a lesbian too. I could just tell by her short hair, and the way she shook my hand.

Which leads me to the next question I know you're thinking about — do I think I'm gonna be a lesbian when I grow up? I don't know. I know my mom wants me to be, even if she doesn't exactly say so. But one night I heard her talking to Linda when she thought I was sleeping. It was pretty easy to listen in on them in the old house because we only had the two rooms. Anyway, it was right after this boy Phillip called me up for the math homework because he was out sick. My mother handed me the phone with this Who's Phillip look in her eye and later that night I heard her talking to Linda.

She said, I hope Ronnie doesn't have to go through her teens and early twenties being straight like I did before she comes out. The thought of adolescent boys running around the house gives me the creeps. I haven't even talked to her about birth control yet. Or AIDS. Oh Goddess — that's what my mom says instead of oh God — Oh Goddess I feel like I just got her out of diapers and already boys are calling her up on the phone.

Then I heard Linda say, relax, Darlin'. Ronnie's got a good head on her shoulders. And besides, we know how to get rid of any fifteen-year-old boys we don't like. We just start with a little of this ... and a little of this ... and before you know it, they'll run home screaming to their mamas. Then I heard my mother laugh — Linda's the only one who can make her laugh — and then they didn't talk any more.

Meanwhile, I didn't bother telling my mother that

Phillip is a real nerd and I wouldn't go out with him if he paid
me a million dollars. Well maybe I would, just once, but he'd
have to put up the money first. In cash. Anyway I wouldn't kiss
him for all the tea in China, like my Aunt Myra would say. I've
never kissed a boy. I've only gone out with a boy once, this guy
Billy from my old school. We went out and he bought me an
ice cream and then he asked if he could kiss me. Kiss me? I
said. Are you kidding? We've only been going out for thirty-
five minutes. We didn't go out again after that.

I don't know, kissing boys seems really gross and
kissing girls seems really weird. Maybe I'll be a nun, except
my mom says Jews can't be nuns. I don't know. I guess I'm
kind of young to worry about it too much. That's what Linda
says anyway. She says just be yourself and see what happens.
I said to her, who else would I be, Whitney Houston and she
laughed — Linda laughs at my jokes most of the time, unlike
my mom.

But really I kind of know what she means, because I
used to pretend I came from a normal family. I even made up
a father and pretended he was away on business trips a lot just
so the other kids wouldn't tease me for being so different and
all. I never told my mom that — I could just imagine what she
would say.

So anyway, that's all about me. I wanted you to know
right off the bat so I wouldn't have to worry about you pulling
a Brenda. Do you think your mom will let us be friends?

Bubbe Meiseh
(Grandmother's Tale)

ELLEN GRUBER GARVEY

ONE OF THE FIRST THINGS Claudia told Jessie about her family was that she had a one-hundred-and-three-year-old grandmother. "All the women in my family live a long time," Claudia said, stretching her long legs across Jessie's kitchen chairs. "It's like my relatives last forever."

It seemed to Claudia that each bit of information about her life dropped loudly into her lover's ears, ringing with significance. "A hundred and three? Your grandmother?" The glint in Jessie's eye was something more than the sparkle of her contact lenses. "I'd love to meet her." Jessie demanded more family stories — a year-by-year account of visits to the grandmother, a tall woman tucked up in quilts in the Bronx, reading the Yiddish paper and issuing trying remarks to her seventy-year-old daughter, Claudia's mother.

Claudia was confident of sharing in her family's tradition of longevity. Her mother, too, would live to be a hundred and three, and seventy years from now Claudia would join the two of them, wrapped in long quilts in the Bronx.

Jessie laughed, pulled her chair closer, and interrupted Claudia's explanation of her prospects for old age to kiss her. She stroked Claudia's hair, twined her fingers through it. "You can see the implications here, can't you?" she said. Why shouldn't her connection to Claudia give her a place in that tradition too? Jessie's own family background — short people living short lives — would unravel; the leftover genetic strands would braid with Claudia's into a net suspended between them. They could lie together in such a hammock for a lifetime — a lifetime of a hundred and three years or longer. With her finger, she drew a hammock on her lover's thigh.

"A one-hundred-and-three-year-old grandma," said Jessie again, her feet dangling above the floor. "Nothing so spectacular in my family. I'd have heard if there was — my mother's always telling what some relative's done. She calls up: 'You'll never guess,' she says, and it turns out a fourth cousin has an article on amniocentesis in a technical journal. I'm supposed to rush out and buy it."

"Ah," said Claudia. "Reflected glory."

"No, not that." Jessie kicked the chair rung. "Some horrible possessive excitement comes over her. She wants it known that she's connected to people who do these things — a heredity that runs backwards, after birth. An umbilical cord made up of phone lines. I hate it."

When Jessie talked about her other relatives, short and numerous, it was Claudia's turn to see implications. Jessie's relatives also lived in the Bronx, not far from Claudia's grandmother in her long quilts. How could it just be neighborhood closeness that made the bad jokes of Jessie's uncles sound as though they could have been embarrassing nieces and nephews in her own family?

"I can't believe it's just from having the Bronx in common," said Claudia. "Your aunts' feuds are exactly the same as my aunts'." She mused over coincidences of names:

23

"Your mother's name is Batya?" she asked. "It's like a mirror image of my family. *I* have a cousin Jessie with a *daughter* named Batya. Always at parties and stuff, in the middle of things. They're very tall, hard to miss."

"That's not like us then. My mother's even shorter than I am," said Jessie. "All these links — it does seem close. Not a mirror though." Jessie laced and unlaced her fingers, thinking. "Maybe there's some hidden connection. A place where a different thread comes in. Like in weaving, when you change the thread on the shuttle —"

"My grandmother talks like that, only with her it's scary connections — conspiracies, webs of intrigue. The Bronx is full of mysterious squads of people out to get her. The entire borough thinks of nothing but her." Claudia shook her finger at Jessie, speaking in a grandmother voice. "It's all connected, you know. You must be very careful." She took back her own voice. "I hate it."

"She could be right. When you read about some of this government corruption — look what's happened to mass transit in the past five or ten years — deferred maintenance —"

"She hasn't been out of the apartment in the past five or ten years, so you can leave that out. She's getting paranoid, that's all. The doctor says hardening of the arteries, but I think she just needs people besides my mother to talk to. She's forgetting her English and my mother's Yiddish isn't so hot."

"You should get students from that Yiddish program at Columbia — they'd probably love to have someone to do oral histories on. Here," Jessie opened a cabinet, dug under a pile of papers, handed Claudia a pamphlet. "The phone number's on the back."

Claudia stared at the earnest faces in the photos, tried to imagine them away from their desks, surrounding her grandmother's long bed. "But it's such a small room. You don't know my grandmother. Don't romanticize this."

*

24

When Jessie's mother introduced herself on the phone one Sunday morning, Claudia naturally recognized the name. Jessie hadn't arrived in the Bronx last night, Batya said. Was she with Claudia? Did Claudia know where she'd gone?

Of course Claudia knew. Saturday night, after dinner and a concert, they'd gone down the subway steps together. Jessie had stopped at the map across from the token booth, standing on tiptoe to trace her route. "BMT, IND, IRT," Claudia had hear her mutter, almost chanting; "not a shuttle exactly." Claudia had watched a sudden smile cross Jessie's face as her finger followed a line of grey shunting to orange, crossing over black, diving under blue: under, over, under. "Such a long trip, though." Jessie's smile had changed to a frown before she shrugged and headed uptown to visit her parents, Claudia back downtown to her own apartment. Jessie had gotten on the train to the Bronx wearing a gray hat and holding the *Times* book review section. Claudia had still been waiting on the downtown platform carrying the rest of the Sunday paper when Jessie's train pulled out of the station.

"She didn't get here," Batya said accusingly. "We found out you saw her last. We don't know where she is." Her voice rose, then dropped to a low whisper: "My cousin has written an article about this sort of thing. He says it happens all the time."

Did they think she was running away? At midnight, her bag packed for the trip to the Bronx, her contact lenses soaking in their case — would she really have changed her mind?

Maybe there'd be a clue in Jessie's apartment. Claudia grabbed her set of keys and took a cab over. Lights were on all over the living room. The contact lens sterilizer sat on a stack of newspapers instead of in its usual place on the coffee table. Jessie must have been there. The short striped scarf Jessie'd woven hung from the doorknob — but she hadn't been wearing that one. Jessie's sister walked in from the next room:

25

It was only the family that had been there, sifting things over. Had they noticed Claudia's blue jeans, so much longer than Jessie's, draped over the chair in the bedroom?

"We still have not heard from her," said Batya, sitting in a low chair in the kitchen, speaking as though only family could have received information. "The police don't know what to think."

Claudia imagined Jessie trapped on a dark Bronx street under the iron lattice pillars of the elevated, unable to find her way. Large men loomed over her, covering her from view; she disappeared completely into the trunk of a car.

Claudia began to sob. Jessie's mother and sister took turns scolding her for being hysterical, with the family so upset. "Not even a relative; what right does she have to take it so hard?" they hissed in the kitchen.

"Don't add to our troubles," said Batya, from the low chair. She looked familiar, and was dressed in black. Perhaps it didn't signify anything — maybe she always wore mourning, always prepared for catastrophe. Jessie had once told her something about that, but Claudia couldn't remember what and now she couldn't ask her.

She ought to tell what Jessie was wearing when last seen. When last seen through the subway car window as the train left for a distant stop in the Bronx, she wore a gray hat and read the book review section. Earlier, Claudia had watched her dress for the visit to her parents, ignoring whatever her mother would have liked to see her in — the skirt and jacket uniform of an office worker riding the subway at rush hour, or heels to make her look taller. Claudia interrogated herself, silently listing the items worn on the subway at midnight: gray hat, theatrical orange shirt, black pants tucked into motorcycle boots, several large-stoned necklaces, a quilted vest. "And what was your overall impression of this outfit, Miss what-did-you-say-your-name-was?" "Exciting, very exciting."

But the police didn't ask her; no one wanted to talk with her. Jessie's mother and sister had spread address books over Jessie's kitchen chairs and were busy calling all the relatives in case they'd heard something. They didn't notice her leave.

Claudia walked down the subway steps alone to follow Jessie's route from the concert hall to the Bronx, pacing each station platform along the way with long strides, peering down among the pillars of the elevated. She stared out the subway car windows as the train went underground again, but couldn't see anything: the dark tunnels turned the glass into a mirror.

Monday, and each morning that week, Claudia tried new routes to the Bronx, pacing platforms, searching among pillars, and posting notices in the streets. Late each afternoon when she returned, she wondered for a moment whether Jessie had gotten back uneventfully but hadn't told her. They hadn't been together that long, after all. Could it be that she'd wanted to break up, and didn't want to say so? Each evening Claudia twisted the phone cord around and around in her hands, calling everyone Jessie had ever mentioned, asking for leads, for help. At the end of each day she fell into bed exhausted with anxiety. But each night when Jessie visited Claudia in her dreams, she appeared free of concern, even pleased with herself, though she never had anything helpful to say when she bent down to kiss Claudia's ear. Each morning Claudia woke feeling somehow encouraged, as though an important memory were about to come to her.

Friday, Claudia's parents invited her to their bungalow colony. "If you haven't found out anything from riding the subway all week, what new are you going to learn today?" said her mother. "Come and rest." Claudia stepped from the train onto the hot sunny path connecting the houses. She opened a screen door and walked through the winding hallways of her

27

family's house. More substantial than one built for a summer resort, covered with Victorian latticework and carpenter's lace, it struck her as a sort of grandmother to the newer, smaller bungalows.

Claudia's mother was in the kitchen talking to a visitor, a short woman in black. The visitor turned as Claudia entered the room, cool and dim after the sun outside. It was Jessie's mother.

"You two know each other?" asked Claudia.

"Oh yes," Claudia's mother put her hand on Batya's shoulder. "We go way back." They'd been socialists together in their youth, she explained. They were discussing the old days.

Batya seemed friendlier than before, smiling at Claudia with crooked teeth. Jessie must be back, Claudia decided, and returned Batya's smile. Jessie would explain what had happened once she saw her. She'd say where she'd been, where the train had left her. It could have been stalled in the narrow space between Manhattan and the Bronx, hidden in a dark tunnel. "Look at the map," she'd point out. "See how little room? I'm surprised it doesn't happen more often." Or she'd tell how, unscheduled and forgotten, the train had slid onto the wrong siding, while the transfer point was misplaced in a change of shifts.

"We still have no word about Jessie," said Batya, smoothing the lap of her black dress, her feet dangling above the floor.

"What does the transit authority say?" asked Claudia. "Maybe the train is still stuck." Claudia understood why Batya had looked familiar; it wasn't just her resemblance to Jessie. She'd seen her picture in an old photo album: Claudia's mother at the beach in the 'thirties, lined up with her friends, arms around one another. "See, there's Estelle with the squint; the tall one in the middle is me; you remember cousin Ruthie;

and the short one in the black bathing suit — that's Batya."

Claudia began to tell her mother what Jessie had been wearing when last seen, when Claudia had looked through the train window to be sure she was safely on her way to her parents in the Bronx. This was probably all Claudia's fault: The surveillance had been too much; Jessie had resented it, felt bound to elude it. Maybe all that close overseeing was what Jessie disliked about her mother's way of collecting relatives' accomplishments. But where would she have gone?

Claudia laced and unlaced her fingers, anxious. She tried to follow her mother's conversation with Batya, lost track of it between twenty years of sectarian groups splintering and the birth of grandchildren. Her eyes drifted up to the subway map tacked to the wall, tried to follow the pathways. A chant began in her head: IRT, IND, BMT.

"How's Grandma?" she broke in.

"Oh, she's making some kind of big fight, she says she doesn't want me coming over all the time, and now her phone's been out all week. You know how impossible she is," her mother said. "Though frankly, it's just as well. The last thing I need right now is more of those remarks coming at me. Besides, we have such a lot to catch up on." She stroked Batya's arm. Batya smiled. "But you, Claudia, you ought to visit her." Claudia's mother looked up at her tall daughter. "You know how much she loves to see you."

"You're absolutely right," said Claudia. "Where's the train schedule?" The two older women walked her back along the sunny connecting pathways to the railroad station. They posed for a new photo: arms around each other, Batya's head level with Claudia's mother's breast. "I have a cousin who makes wonderful photographs," said Batya. "Very prominent." Claudia snapped the picture from the train. Three stations later, she made the right connection to the subway, and traced her route: over, under, over. She arrived at her

29

grandmother's building, and opened the apartment door.

The gray hat hung in the foyer. The boots had been kicked down the hallway. Large-stoned necklaces were hooked on the bedroom doorknob. Jessie was under the quilt with Grandma, each reading a section of the Yiddish paper.

"It's about time," said her grandmother to Claudia. "You don't know how to get to your own grandma's anymore? We were starting to worry."

"It took a while to make the right connection," said Claudia.

"Come." Her grandmother smiled with crooked teeth. "You remember Batya's daughter Jessie, don't you?"

"Of course," said Claudia. Jessie wiggled her toes, which now stuck out from the bottom of the long quilt. She handed Claudia the book review section of the Yiddish paper.

"Well, get in then," said her grandmother.

Letter from the Warsaw Ghetto

SUSAN RUTH GOLDBERG

24 April 1943
Warsaw Ghetto

DEAR CHANA,

If you are still alive now I do not have to describe to you what is around me — you will be seeing it too. We move quickly from roof to roof, just ahead of the fires, and have settled for what may be hours or perhaps the rest of the night in a spot that seems relatively safe for the moment, the roof of Pawia 37. The ghetto is burning everywhere — are you out there somewhere, Chana, on another roof, or down in a bunker? Are your eyes taking this in anymore, or are you gone from this world? I have heard nothing of you since the beginning of this — going on to five days now. No one has any news of you or the others in your group.

Our numbers are greatly reduced. Yossi is dead, so are Freydl and Yitzhak, also Michl and Itka. We are exhausted and cold, our lungs are sore from smoke, our eyes and noses are burning. We are exhilarated, though, over each victory, each day that we manage to survive. When we are fighting I am not afraid — only later, when we stop, when we have time to think, like now. Then fear overwhelms me in a wave that threatens to drown me, and I must struggle through it, as though I were really gagging and choking and swallowing water, into a lighter air, and find something to hold on to, to focus on, so that I can push the fear back down again, contain it.

So often what I find myself holding to is my image of your face, your clear, beautiful eyes regarding me solemnly. If only we were still together, if only we hadn't been assigned to different fighting groups, if only I could see you now, hear your calm voice, touch your hand, know that you are not dead. The worst is to not know if you are dead, to not know if I am talking to you or to your memory. I guess I do know, though, that no matter what, I am writing a letter that will never be mailed, that you will probably never read. Maybe that's why I'm writing it now, when I know you will never see it, the only way I can ever say these things to you.

I don't know what these feelings are, if they have come to me because of how we have lived since we have known each other, in these unreal times, always with death and fear and hunger and loss, or if they would have come no matter how or when I met you. But here, in the bizarre extremities of existence that we have been forced to call our life, here is where I came to know you and to experience, secret to myself, feelings of such joy and intensity when I am around you that I have had to give them the name of love. I have not had such depth or strength of feeling for any young man, ever. Sometimes I have been frightened by the power of these emotions, especially by an almost physical sensation of longing that accompanies them. Usually, though, I have found in them a source of confidence and happiness and hope, and if I have been frightened by my own feelings, I have *never* been frightened by *you* — only enriched and buoyed and encouraged by your presence — by your will and your spirit, your courage and faith. I know that in this hell we have been the luckiest — those of us finally able to fight, to work alongside friends in resistance, and I, to have known you, to have felt love, though I can only now express it; to have thrown a grenade at the Germans, though I shall probably die tomorrow.

Now, because you are not here, I fantasize the bravery that I would have to have to say these things to you. What would you say? Would you laugh at me, recoil, tell me that this war has made me mad? Or just pushed me to an extreme from which I will recede, if we survive? Might you hear me truly, and respond? I won't know, will I? If we live, if we survive, if we meet tomorrow or next year, will I ever speak these words to you? We have all fought so long to survive, to tell the world what has happened to us, and now, at last, to know that we will die resisting, that it is all we know. Can we believe in, can we picture a future? I cannot anymore; my future is now, it is tomorrow morning when the Germans come back into the Ghetto at first light. Everything that I have lived and felt and thought is focused on right now, where I must concentrate all my energy, all my Jewish being, all my love for you, another Jewish woman huddled out there in the night on a burning roof with her gun; or dead, dead . . . oh, Chana, not dead. There is only now, this moment, it is all that is real. I send my love out to you through the Ghetto, wherever you are, through time, where you are. All love.

Teibl

Nicholas

HARRIET MALINOWITZ

"SURPRISE," I SAY.

It is.

For Nicholas is the last thing my mother expected, and I know that even in this first second she's seeing him wrong. I know what she thinks; I know how babies look through her eyes. She has no inkling of what he really is. I know I have the winning card in hand, to use whenever I want. I know. And she doesn't.

I tip the wheel of the stroller up the step into the livingroom, and lift him out, into my arms. I see her watching, hungrily, and I clutch him tightly to me. She is puzzled, distant, eager to reach for him, but my arms around him barricade her out. I possess him. She doesn't.

It is September, 1977, the month of my twenty-third birthday. In the East Village it is a cool, cloudy Wednesday afternoon. In my mother's house in Queens it is verging on Yom Kippur, the Jewish day of atonement.

I have just taken a subway ride from Second Avenue, with Nicholas. On the train I sat in an aisle seat, with the stroller parked, brake on, beside me. I held onto it with one hand, while Nicholas dozed, drugged by the rhythm of the train. At Thirty-Fourth Street I looked up and saw Howard Weintraub hanging from a strap halfway down the car. He saw me at the same moment. We haven't seen each other since our graduation from high school five years ago, and after the first start of recognition had crossed his face there was a second shock, as he gaped at me and then Nicholas and back at me again. He pointed with his finger, his eyebrows lifting in amazement. I shook my head, laughing, and his shoulders heaved in mock relief before he pushed his way toward me. The second after I'd shaken my head no I wished I'd nodded instead, just for fun. Howard was dressed in a brown suit and tie, and he carried a briefcase. The first thing he said, after five years, was: "Going home for the holiday?" He told me he was an accountant and was getting married in June. I told him I was doing street theater satirizing capitalist patriarchy, and I explained about Nicholas. I saw a look of groping incertitude come to Howard's face that I'd never seen there once in four years of high school. I enjoyed the contrast between us. Very much.

This is the year I have decided to eclipse Yom Kippur. For years it has dragged me back, like childhood, an encumbrance that can't be shrugged off, or shed like a dead skin, so I could keep on metamorphizing. It doesn't matter if I travel to the ends of the earth, write great manifestoes, sleep with women, confront head-on the hells that lurk behind the stolid doorways of life; September still always comes and strips me of my guts, sucking me deep into its belly like a high-speed vacuum cleaner.

Obviously, I haven't been able to avoid it this year, for I am here. But if Yom Kippur can intrude on me, so can I intrude on Yom Kippur. I have come, but Nicholas has come with me; and now I stand in the livingroom of my mother's house, which I still have to take care not to refer to accidentally as "my" house, with my arms protecting Nicholas, and Nicholas's small body protecting me.

"What's this?" exclaims my mother at last.

"A baby," I answer her.

She squints at me, drawing her head back a little.

"*Whose* baby?" she persists.

"A friend's," I say, sitting down in the rocker still wrapped in my woolen poncho, and beginning to rock to and fro with Nicholas in my lap, his deep brown eyes gazing into mine and mine into his. "A friend who's in the hospital. I *told* you I was bringing a surprise home for the holiday. Aren't you surprised?"

"I certainly am!" she agrees. Her irony is mixed with excitement. "Here, let me take him . . ."

"It's OK, I've got him," I say, raising my elbow just in time to block her.

"What's his name?" she asks hurt, and hovering closely by at a loss, probably because no one has ever before challenged her in the realm of babies.

"Nicholas," I say. Just then Nicholas smiles at me, perhaps from hearing his own name, and I smile back.

"If your friend is in the hospital, where is Nicholas's father? Or shouldn't I ask?"

"You can ask," I say generously. "Nicholas's father is in Angola."

She is silent a moment.

"What is he doing in Angola, with a helpless infant and a wife in the hospital? Or — not a wife, maybe," she amends, almost apologetically, as if she knows me too well and is venturing this liberal hypothesis so I won't get my back up.

"He's a revolutionary," I reply.

Her eyes narrow. "Oh, and while he's busy starting the revolution it's OK for him to forget about his responsibilities to his child, and to his — I don't know her name, your friend —"

"He has no responsibilities to them. He has nothing to do with Nicholas's life. Ellen is essentially a single parent, if you must know." Of course she must know. Haven't I brought Nicholas here to prove it?

She grimaces and makes a sound to indicate her conviction that someone's personal craziness has been carried too far; that it is all very well to be idealistic and invent new ideas about families and relationships and children, but not to the point where you're actually tampering with *reality* — the kind of reality that is sitting in my lap in the rocking chair. I know that she is thinking this. I know she thinks Nicholas is the fruit of two overgrown children who have played with concepts that have nothing to do with what life is *really* about.

"And your friend — Ellen — has no family she can leave him with? Some familiar people who will care for him?"

"Her family is in St. Louis, and I'm more familiar to him than they are anyway. I'm perfectly capable of caring for him, or else I wouldn't have taken him."

"Couldn't her mother have flown in? I'm sure, if she knew her daughter was going into the hospital and the baby getting passed around from hand to hand . . ."

"He's not getting passed around! He's with *me*! Besides, Ellen hasn't told her about the surgery. It's not a really big deal, and she hardly ever speaks to her, anyway."

"She hardly speaks to her mother?"

"That's right."

She pauses; then: "I'm *sure* her parents would want to know, especially if it concerned the welfare of their grandchild." Again, a beyond-all-shadow-of-a-doubt conviction.

"Anyway, they don't, and it's her decision."

She shakes her head. "It's pathetic," she says. I don't know if she means *it,* the situation, or *him,* in the dehumanizing way people sometimes speak of babies, but suddenly my anger turns to shame, my defiance to helplessness, and I quickly pass him to her. I cannot rid myself of him quickly enough. Suddenly, relegated to pathos, he feels like a contaminating substance in my arms and I need to make myself clean. "Here," I say, roughly, trying to press down the nausea that is welling inside me. I want to say, "There was no need to call him pathetic, but if you bring that up then you have to take responsibility for it."

But once he is in her arms, I see with mingled anger and relief, she is making him into an acceptable baby. She talks to him in her language, and he likes it. He smiles and gurgles appreciatively. I feel a little jealous that they are communicating so well. And a little outraged, that a baby of his origins could capitulate so easily! But I watch, waiting for her to do or say something that will retract what she has said before: "I was wrong — he's not pathetic, after all!" She is taking such obvious pleasure in holding him that I feel this is established.

She returns him to me so that she can heat up his milk. I hold him more comfortably now; things are a little clearer now. I want to remove my poncho and gently, carefully, I place him on the sofa. I slip the woolen folds over my head and quickly, quickly move to the closet, not removing my eyes for a second yet feeling wrong —

"*Shelley!*" I know this tone. I know what it means and it confirms what I have been feeling wrong about for these last few seconds. I am filled with anger — hopeless, impotent rage that I have brought Nicholas here to help me express, only apparently that was a mistake, too, for she has taken him from the sofa. She is armed; I'm not.

"You don't leave a baby alone on a sofa!" she says, and I say, "*You* don't!" and she says, exasperatedly, "Oh, *Shelley!*" I want to cry, "You see! You see! I'm sure you never left *me* on a sofa, and that's why I'm afraid of everything!" but then

I realize you can't say things like that, and I wonder how I can make her see it without saying it. I can't. Instead, she is making *me* see; I am feeling sick and miserable about the careless thing I have just done so deliberately.

The relatives come and they are delighted with Nicholas. "Who is he?" they want to know, and I feel censorious waves emanating from my mother — who is in the kitchen, arranging chopped eggs and onions inside a circle of Tam Tams on a plate — telling me not to defile the healthy Jewish holiday atmosphere with the truth about Nicholas. I explain, scrupulously honest, that Ellen met Nicholas's father, a Brazilian, in Portugal during the revolution in 1975; and that she became pregnant on purpose and wrote to him from New York, asking him how he would feel knowing he had a child whose life he would have no part in. He wrote back that he felt fine about it. She had the baby in her Soho loft with a midwife and me there to help.

I make it clear that Ellen has freely chosen all this.

As my relatives digest this information, I decide to stop and leave it at that. They are looking at me in the way they sometimes do when I am not yielding to their mentalities. There is a puzzled look in their eyes that distances them from me, that makes me feel a great gulf between us. I have purposely created this gulf, yet I am suddenly seized by an unreasonable desire to swim it. I look from face to face, cringing at the baffled disapproval I see. When I glance at my aunt Sarah I am startled to see awe in her expression. This is the triumph I have been looking for, yet it disturbs me. Perhaps I don't want to be taken seriously after all? Perhaps I want to be convinced, like the rest of them, that the world of Nicholas is just an imaginary world? But no, then I'm wrong again, and Nicholas is here to help me put an end to being wrong like this all the time.

Dinner is over; everyone has begun fasting. They will

fast until three stars appear in the sky tomorrow night. I let it slip, accidentally on purpose, that I will not fast. I'll humor them, as I have always been urged to do, and pretend to fast, yet it is understood that when no one is looking I will eat. Nicholas begins to cry. Everyone wants to hold him. Everyone thinks she has the magic touch, the special comfort to quiet him. After he has screamed for half an hour they lose patience, and I find that I have him all to myself. I take him in the den and pace up and down the room, jostling and soothing him. He does not stop. I check his diaper; he is dry, but there is a massive redness between his legs where inexperienced hands have fastened the diaper so that it chafes. I remove the diaper and rub in ointment. Everyone piles into the den, making silly sounds, and he lies there happy in his nakedness, giggling up at the looming faces. He is not circumcised. "He doesn't realize that this is probably the only Yom Kippur he'll ever have," someone says. As if hereafter he will be deprived.

In spite of this, I feel happy now. I feel like the happy vortex, the point where east meets west, where Nicholas meets my family. This disappears when my mother gathers him once again into her arms and says with a renewed note of chagrin, "The poor thing!"

"*Stop* that!" I cry passionately. "He's fine! There's nothing wrong with him!" But my stomach has begun to lurch again. I wish I had never done this. I don't want to hear my mother's voice but I am helpless to erase it; like a black box intact after an explosion it remains with me, intransigent against time, against soul.

The Lamp:
A Parable About Art and Class and the Function of Kishinev in the Jewish Imagination

IRENA KLEPFISZ

In 1903, a pogrom in Kishinev (Bessarabia) resulted in the death of forty-five Jews. News of the pogrom evoked mass protests in England and the U.S.

I HAVE A LAMP that two of my friends deem unbearable. It's tall and leans unforgivingly. The pole is loose in the plastic marble mooring. Its faded, dusty lampshade won't stay put because a screw is missing. It looks like a scarecrow that lost its arms and straw during a pogrom. And there it stands, right in my livingroom.

An artist friend of mine finds it repulsive. She, not surprisingly, is obsessed with aesthetics. It's a way of life. She's an artist always and finds the lamp intensely disturbing. She keeps asking me how I can bear to look at it all day. I laugh, never having given it a second thought. Once she stayed in my place while I was away. When I got back the lamp was missing. She'd shoved it into one of my closets. I immediately took it out and put it back in its place by the open window where I often sit and read.

Another friend hates my lamp because it reeks from poverty and what she thinks is indulgence — the yellow lampshade I refuse to clean up, the pole which I won't ground.

To this friend, environment is self. She builds and rebuilds her apartment, paints her bookshelves then strips them, reviews her livingroom trying to find the one piece of furniture that could be dumped or replaced to make it all fall into place like a certain Cezanne painting she so admires. She wants to be able to sit in a room of her own creation and feel herself come together in a unified whole.

Such an attitude brings only disaster whenever she visits. She shudders at the rusted shower stall, at the misplaced furniture. Why isn't my desk at the window instead of in the darkest corner? Why is the bookcase free-standing and not anchored to the wall? And that lamp! Why keep it? It looks like a scarecrow. This whole place, she tells me, looks like Kishinev after the pogrom.

But as I try to explain, the lamp is the least of my worries. I'm already middle-aged and still unsettled. I still live alone with no illusions about finding a lover. I still have no steady work or profession. I'm not romantic about my poverty. I don't feel indulgent. My material circumstances feel terminal. *I* feel terminal. On the other hand, I think about the poor people living on the street or people living without heat or water in burnt out buildings, and I feel lucky. This time it's not me. My place's got heat, no leaks. I've managed to pay my bills. The electricity is on and so is the gas. It could be worse. It has been.

Besides, lately I feel like I'm a marathon runner heading full speed towards my cemetery plot in New Jersey. Time is going right past me or I'm rushing past it. Should I stop and shop around for a lamp? Maybe if I ran across one, just by accident, and it was real cheap, I might consider it. Maybe. It's not that I don't care for material things. There are many things I lust for. For example, pens, colored paper. I also covet books and am adept at switching labels when the price is way out of line and I grow indignant. So I'd much rather buy pens or paper or a used book than a lamp, especially a lamp which would only substitute for one that is working full well. And the lamp *is* working. The wiring is fine. Why *not* keep it?

As for the aesthetic argument . . . Well, I'll confess, I have a weakness — let's just say I'm always more forgiving with artists. A wrong line to them is real grief. They can't help it. Who understands these things? I'm sure if this lamp were the only source of evening light, my artist friend wouldn't have shoved it in the closet. But it wasn't. So by hiding the lamp she was doing exactly what I do by keeping it out. It's a question of visions. She's a painter. And I — to my life's joy — am a poet.

Of course, there are other differences between us. She's not a Jew. And this too is important: we're at opposite ends of the spectrum when it comes to light. To me light is merely a means — to read a page from a book, to write a line of a poem. But it is in darkness that my poems come to me. It is in darkness my imagination finds comfort. Now to my artist friend, light is essence. She clings to natural light, refusing to turn on any lamp until the last ray of sun has disappeared. Shade and color are all of life to her. I seek out dark corners and words to release me. Still, we understand each other. After all, we're both poor and that helps.

As for my other friend — we share five thousand years of history. Yet I can't make her understand that I'm getting closer and closer to New Jersey and there are certain things it would be stupid to stop for. Besides it's all more than my grandmother had, more than my grandmother ever hoped for. With poems, it's more than enough for me. Perhaps it's the collective memory of Kisinev. I don't know. I do know it's been worse, much worse.

The Trouble
with Theaters

JUDY FREESPIRIT

MALKA LAY STRETCHED out on her back, watching the sunset through the wide windows of her bedroom. The Sunday evening sky was heavy with dark clouds, sporting bright orange underbellies. She watched the colors changing as the sun dipped slowly into the Bay just a mile away. It felt good, lying there absentmindedly stroking the brown flannel sheets, thinking about how much pleasure she got from her apartment. Malka felt a kind of safety just having this place of her own. It was some comfort after all and she needed comforting tonight. This time of her life seemed more alone than any she could remember. It was an aloneness that was jarring and unexpected. Her life had seemed so full of friends and lovers and chosen "family" that she could hardly believe it could all seem so empty so suddenly, and for such an unexpected reason.

It began quite simply, just two days earlier, when she decided she wanted to go to the Jewish Film Festival that was being held for one week in San Francisco and the following week in Berkeley. That was all. A simple thing, most people would think. Last year she had wanted to go too, and the year before that, but she had dismissed the idea because she was too ill those years. Back then she couldn't have dealt with the hassle of confronting the organizers about the access barriers that existed for fat and disabled people. The theaters they were using for the events had teeny tiny seats and no space for wheelchairs. There had been a time years ago when she was willing and able to squeeze into those tight little seats and suffer the pain and consequent bruises they caused, but not anymore. Now she decided she would just carry a folding chair into the theater, and convince the theater people that she had a right to be there.

She needed to have a space in which to put the chair, that was all there was to it. The metal folding chair would be cold, uncomfortable and conspicuous in the theater aisle, but she could manage if only there was a flat space to put it in. Some theaters were on a downward slope, she had discovered, and a chair that was not bolted down would tilt forward. It was an impossible situation. So having decided that she would find some way to go to the Festival the task was to get the information she needed about what physical barriers she would have to deal with.

On Friday morning she had begun making the necessary telephone calls:

10:00 a.m. The man's voice was cheerful and animated. "You have reached the Reno Four Cinema. We are located at 8844 Hillman at 7th in Berkeley. Today we are playing . . ." Malka listened to the whole spiel which included the information that there would indeed be a Jewish Film Festival in Theater One, and that for further information she could call 555-7676. When she called there was no answer.

10:05 a.m. She dialed the office of the Jewish Film Festival. The woman on the answering machine was energetic and had just a hint of New York in her voice. "The Jewish Film

45

Festival continues at the Sands Theater in San Francisco through August 23rd." *(This was on the 24th of August!)* "There are plenty of tickets left for all shows, but come 30 minutes early to get good seats. Sorry, but there are no reservations." The tape clicked off. Nothing about the showings in the East Bay. Nothing about when they might be in the office or how to get information about future showings. Just a click.

10:10 a.m. Malka dialed the Jewish Museum where her friend Lila worked. It was a kindly, older woman's voice which answered, this time in person. "Jewish Museum," she said sweetly.

"Hi, may I speak with Lila Shapiro?"

"I'm sorry, but she doesn't work on Fridays. Can someone else help you?"

"Oh, well . . . ah . . . do you have a phone number for the Jewish Film Festival office that isn't a recording, where I can get a real person to talk to?"

"Just a moment — I'll check." The pause seemed awfully long.

Why is everything always so damned hard? Malka wondered.

The voice returned. "The number is 555-2288."

"That's the number of the recording. Don't you have another number for them?"

The woman seemed genuinely sympathetic when she answered, "I'm sorry. That's the only one we have."

At 11:15 Malka decided to try the Reno Theater again. Still no answer.

11:20 a.m. She called the festival office and got the same machine message.

2:00 p.m. It occurred to Malka that the Jewish Federation Council in Oakland might have some information. They were sympathetic, but said that the only number they had was the one on which she had been getting the recording. Another strike-out.

2:07 p.m. She decided to try the Reno again. This time a loud male voice answered with something that sounded like, "Horeno."

"Is this the Reno Theater?"

"Yeah."

"I have a question . . ."

"Is it about the Jewish Festival?"

"Well, not exactly. It's about seating space. I need to know if you have any wheelchair space where I can put a chair."

"No, we can't have no chairs in the aisles. It's gonna be real crowded."

Malka winced at the gruffness of his voice. It made her feel like a little child, being yelled at by a grownup. She gritted her teeth before speaking. "You mean there will be no disabled seating?"

"No, we are told to discourage anybody in wheelchairs. It's gonna be crowded and the Fire Department will be here and we can't have nobody blocking the exits."

"Do you usually have wheelchair space in the theater?"

"Yeah, but like I told ya not for this festival. It's gonna be real crowded and we're supposed to discourage wheelchairs. I'm only the janitor, but that's what they told us."

By this time Malka's body felt like it was made of knots and her jaw seemed locked tight. She could hardly keep from screaming at the man, but she managed to ask, "Who told you that, the theater people or the festival people?"

"Both," he answered.

"I see," Malka nearly yelled into the phone, "so disabled people aren't welcome." She slammed the receiver hard on the cradle, forgetting that she was at her desk at work, then looked around quickly and was relieved to see that nobody working nearby had noticed.

4:15 p.m. After a number of other calls to the Festival office with no better results she finally phoned Lila at her home. Lila listened to her story and said that she had the phone number of one of the women on the committee. "Call me Monday morning at the Museum and I'll see what I can do."

Well, that was all she could do for the time being, but she felt on the verge of tears, and snapped at people for the rest of the afternoon. She even felt like punching her supervisor several times, but managed to restrain herself.

That had been on Friday and now, this beautiful Sunday evening, Malka didn't feel like punching anyone. The clouds were now nearly devoid of their pink glow, and were a deep, almost navy blue. "How would Esther describe this sunset?" she wondered. Esther would have said it in some beautifully poetic way, she was sure. It was a mystery to Malka how Esther was able to use words. She rolled over on her side, still facing the window, wrapped her arms around the soft flannel-covered pillow, and thought about her friend.

Esther had come over late Saturday afternoon to pick up Monique who was visiting from Montreal. Monique, a fat, French Canadian dyke, had wanted to meet all the fat dykes in town, and especially Malka, whom she had heard speak on a panel four years earlier. So Esther introduced them and Monique and Malka spent a lovely day together, having breakfast, going swimming, then back to Malka's apartment where they talked non-stop. The day sped by so quickly that when Esther showed up to get Monique, the women were amazed.

"Is it really that late?" Malka asked as Esther came into the apartment.

"Sure, it's five o'clock. You two look like you've been having a good time." Esther sat down in the wicker-backed rocker in the livingroom, smiling at her two friends who had obviously been enjoying each other's company.

Monique's smile was broad and warm. "I'm very glad we had a chance to get to talk," she told Malka. "I'm sorry we didn't have more time. I'm leaving in two days. It seems like we just started to get to know each other."

"Well, we'll just have to do it again sometime," Malka answered. "What are you two doing this evening?"

"Oh, we're just going to have dinner at my house and maybe make a fire in the fireplace," Esther replied. "Oh, by the way, I won't be at the Jewish lesbian writer's group meeting next week. I'm going to the Jewish Film Festival that night."

Malka's body tensed and her teeth clenched. "That damned Festival," she sputtered. "I spent hours yesterday trying to get information about the seating space. It was awful."

Esther nodded. "I know a lot of fat dykes who are really discouraged with it. They fought with the organizers last year and finally got to take in their own chairs, but Rebecca isn't even going this year because she doesn't want to have to fight again to get in. She won't even talk to me about it."

"How can you go then, when . . ." Malka began, astonished, then stopped short.

"Go ahead," Esther pursued, "what were you going to say?"

"Aren't you and Rebecca still lovers?" she asked.

"Yes." Esther's voice was subdued. She knew what was coming next.

Malka could not control the anger in her voice. "Well, I just can't understand how you can go to the festival when your lover can't even get in!"

Esther became very quiet. In fact all three of the women sat in shocked silence which seemed to fill the whole room.

"I'm not in a position to struggle with the Festival

organizers." Esther's voice was barely audible. "I don't have the energy to change things everywhere I go. I don't know if this is a priority for me."

Then another silence hung heavily over them. Malka felt as if the walls were closing in on her. She was having trouble breathing and she wanted more than anything else for this to be over. She thought about saying something that would make Esther feel better, get her off the hook, but she didn't really want to let her off so easily. Malka just sat there, looking at Esther, hoping she would leave soon. She was just too confused. She didn't know Monique well enough to be having such an emotional scene in front of her she thought, then realized that wasn't true. Monique was understanding everything that was happening. The tension was becoming unbearable as the three women sat silently, each unable to move and each unable or unwilling to do anything to make things feel better.

Esther finally broke the silence. "I don't know what to say," she said. "I don't feel good about leaving like this. I feel so . . . unfinished." Her large brown eyes spoke her pain more eloquently than her words.

Malka didn't know what to say either. She shrugged helplessly, as if to say, "Me too, I don't know what to do either."

When Esther finally stood up she still didn't move toward the door, but stood looking at Malka with a pained expression. Malka stared at the carpet, and Monique looked back and forth between the two friends, sympathy on her face and a quiet tension in her body. At last Esther moved toward Malka and hugged her hard. "I'll talk to you soon," she said.

Malka responded with a long hug. "Have a good evening with Monique." Then she and Monique embraced affectionately. "I'm really glad we got to spend the day together. Next time I'm in Montreal I'll let you know and we can hang out again."

Monique laughed. "Well," she said, "I'll be back next year in case you don't make it to Montreal before then, and we'll see each other then." They embraced again and Malka walked the two of them to the door. As she was leaving Esther turned and gave Malka a small wave, the way a child would, holding her hand in the air and bending her four fingers several times. Then they were gone.

The sobs wrenched Malka's body as the tears, which had been welling just on the edge of her eyes, spilled over and flowed down her cheeks. As she threw herself on the bed and pounded the mattress with her fists she felt first confused, then angry, then suddenly she stopped as the realization hit her. She was totally alone in this battle. All her friends, even her lovers and closest friends went to the movies. They knew she couldn't go because the seats were too small. Each of the past two years, and this one as well, they had all gone off to the Jewish Film Festival as well as the regular movies she would have liked to see. Nobody had confronted the theater owners or offered to. Nobody boycotted the theaters because their friend couldn't go. They all knew how badly Malka felt about being excluded, and each had commiserated and then gone off to the movies without her.

Despite her righteous anger over their recent interaction, Malka realized she was also feeling badly about the way she had treated Esther. The anger was valid but Esther wasn't her enemy. She was a fat woman too, not as fat as Malka, but fat enough to have problems with other people's attitudes. She had been unfair dumping all her anger on this friend, when Esther was no worse than all the other women who claimed they loved her and still left her stranded while they went merrily off to the theater. Once again Malka's tears burst to the surface and she pummelled the bed and sobbed until she finally became exhausted. Then she lay quietly for a long time planning the call she would make to Lila on Monday morning.

>*"Hi Lila, I just wanted to ask you to do me a favor."*
>*"Sure, what is it?"*
>*"Well, if you have the number of that woman on the Film Festival Committee would you please give her a message for me?"*
>*"Sure, what is it?"*
>*"Tell her that I'll be there tonight with a chair, and I'm coming in one way or another. And tell her if she wants to be sure that next year there's not a boycott with fat and disabled picketers outside the theater she should call me so we can get it clear what the Committee has to do to avoid a major financial and cultural disaster."*
>*"Sure, Malka. I think you're right about all this and you have my support. There's no reason why they couldn't have found some theater that's accessible by the third year of the Festival. There's no excuse for it. Just let me know if there's anything you want from me and I'll do what I can."*
>*"Thanks Lila, and let's hope we don't have to organize around this. I've got a lot of things I'd rather be doing with my time."*

This fantasy stuff is fun, Malka decided, as she turned on the radio. Soft music was just what she needed for the next round of planning.

>*There is a line outside the theater. Malka is in line alone, right near the front. She has planned it that way so she can be there to block the rest of the line if they will not let her in. She places her money in the ticket taker's window and says, "One please." The ticket taker notices the folding chair she is carrying and says, "You can't take that into the theater."*
>*Malka: Why not?*

Ticket Taker: Because we're not allowed to have anyone sitting in the aisles.

Malka: Then can you please direct me to a seat which is large enough?

Ticket Taker: Uh, aren't the seats big enough?

Malka: No, I've been here before and they're definitely too small for me.

Ticket Taker: "Well, could you please step aside so I can take care of these other people and you can talk to the manager."

Malka: No, I won't step aside. If I can't go in nobody is going in. (She takes her chair and opens it, sitting down right in front of the ticket window.)

Ticket Taker: Hey, you can't sit there.

Malka: Really?

Manager: What's going on here? What's the trouble?

Ticket Taker: She wants to take her chair into the theater because she's too big for our seats. . . .

Malka: The seats are too small for me.

Manager: Please come over here while we work this out.

Malka: I'm not going anywhere until I get a ticket and you show me a place where I can put my chair inside the theater.

Manager: If you don't move I'll have to call the police.

Malka: We all have to do what we have to do.

People in Line: Hey, what's the holdup? We want to get into the theater. It's almost time for the show to start. What's going on? (etc.)

Manager: (to the crowd) Please be patient and we'll have this cleared up in just a few minutes. (turning to Malka) Look lady, be reasonable. You're keeping all these people from going into the show.

*Malka: And **you're** keeping **me** from going into the*

show.

>   *Manager: Listen, you're holding things up. We have a show coming up in just a few minutes.*

>   *Malka: Then I guess you'd better find some way for me to be seated so we can get on with the show.*

>   *Manager: I'm calling the police. (he leaves)*

A few minutes pass and two uniformed Berkeley police officers arrive.

>   *First Officer: What's the problem here?*

>   *Manager: This woman is blocking the ticket window and won't let anyone in.*

>   *Second Officer: Sorry lady, but you'll have to move or we'll have to take you in.*

>   *Malka: (no response)*

>   *First Officer: Come on now, be reasonable. You're keeping all these people from buying their tickets. You're causing a public nuisance. I can throw a lot of charges at you, but it takes a lot of paper work, so if you'll just move on we can forget the whole thing.*

>   *Malka: (no response)*

>   *Second Officer: (to Manager) Do you want to press charges?*

>   *Manager: Well, if she won't move I guess I'll have to.*

>   *Second Officer: OK, lady, what's your name?*

>   *Malka: (no response)*

>   *Second Officer: You're going to have to come with us to the police station. (As they grab her arms, Malka goes limp and slumps in her chair.)*

>   *First Officer: Oh shit. How are we going to carry her? She must weigh 300 pounds.*

>   *Malka: 330.*

>   *First Officer: (pleading) Be reasonable lady.*

>   *Malka: (no response)*

>   *(Huffing and puffing as they go, the two officers carry*

her out to the squad car.)

Malka lay smiling silently in the now darkened bedroom. What a scene that will be, she thought. Then she got up
and undressed in the dark. It was early to go to sleep, but she
wanted to get to bed early tonight. Tomorrow was going to be
one hell of a day.

The temperature was still in the low 90s as Malka
hauled her kitchen chair the two blocks from her parked car to
the Reno Theater. When she reached the end of the long line
of people waiting to purchase tickets she put down the chair
and sat with a sigh. Each time the line moved she scooted the
chair forward. When she was almost to the door she decided
to stand and carry it the rest of the way. The young man
standing at the door didn't seem to notice her at all. So far so
good. The lobby was crowded with people, some buying
popcorn and candy, others just standing around and talking.
Malka scanned the lobby and found what she was looking for;
two women wearing badges which read JEWISH FILM
FESTIVAL STAFF.

"I'd like to know where's the best place to put my chair
in the theater," she said firmly. "Is there a flat area where I can
sit?"

"Sure," said the shorter woman. "Come on in and I'll
show you where the disabled area is. You can put the chair
there with no problem."

It was just that easy. No struggle, no demonstration.
Just a nice pleasant Jewish woman being helpful. Malka felt
disappointed. On one hand it was great that she didn't have to
fight to get access. On the other she was angry that they were
acting as if they intended to be accommodating, as if it had
been assumed all along that she could be seated. She had been
ready for a fight. Now she felt cheated and conspicuous, as she

sat alone in the area separated from the rows of regular seats.

"Oy vey," she laughed to herself. "Some people are never satisfied."

Smiling at her own joke, Malka shifted her weight and got as comfortable as she could on a kitchen chair. Then the lights dimmed and so did some of her pain, as she immersed herself in the drama on the screen.

Crisis

JYL LYNN FELMAN

LAST WEEK Edith Rebecca Greenblatt unplugged her phone. She had been in severe psychic pain for weeks. She did not want to see anyone, not even her girlfriend, Hilda Schwartz. Edith did not know where the pain had come from. She wondered if the pain was Jewish because she had finally cut herself off from the *goyim*. But then Schwartzie couldn't get through either.

Wednesday night after plugging her phone back in, Edith picked up the receiver and asked for help. She called Alice Blakely, a name she had picked from an alphabetical list of local therapists in the yellow pages. There had been nine women listed as professional therapists, but only Alice Blakely had had an opening this week. Edith swallowed hard before telling her new therapist that she was a lesbian. She had coughed and couldn't get the words out when she tried to tell the woman that she was a Jew. An appointment was set for 9:15, Friday morning. Edith hoped she could wait that long. When she put the receiver down, she unplugged the phone.

Friday morning, she drove slowly. How was she going

to explain her condition to a total stranger? Edith wanted to be specific. I'm in crisis, seemed a good place to start. Turning onto Wild Knoll Drive, she counted the houses. One, two, it was the third blue house on the left. A huge German Shepherd came leaping out from the side of the house, ready to pounce on Edith as soon as she opened the door. It was definitely insensitive to have a barking dog leaping out at your clients.

As soon as she turned the motor off, Edith noticed that the dog stopped moving. The least Alice could have done was warn her. She got out of the car without taking her eyes off the animal and continued staring at him until she reached the side of the house. Nothing happened. Edith opened the door and sat down on the couch. She was in a waiting room.

The dog had slowed her down; it was already ten after nine. She needed the extra few minutes to think about what she was going to say. I've been depressed for a long time, sounded better than I'm in crisis. After all she didn't have any real proof of her depression except that she had unplugged her phone. She didn't know what was wrong with her, but her relationship with Schwartzie was absolutely not the issue. If there was one thing Edith Rebecca Greenblatt knew about herself, it was that she loved loving Jewish women. Even that didn't sound right.

On the table next to the couch she noticed several diplomas in cheap black frames. They were stacked one on top of the other like magazines in her dentist's office. Edith had never seen diplomas displayed that way. She picked up the top one. ALICE BLAKELY IS HEREBY AWARDED A MASTER OF SCIENCES DEGREE IN SOCIAL WORK. *Social Work.* Alice had said nothing on the phone about what Edith called social working. Edith pictured herself talking to someone who went into people's homes looking for poverty and child abuse. She could almost hear the woman's soft knock on the inner city door, her arms full of Shop & Save groceries. Edith knew she needed a therapist, not a saint.

She continued reading, THE TOWN OF CONWAY, NEW

HAMPSHIRE, HEREBY AWARDS ALICE BLAKELY A CITATION FOR EXCELLENCE IN HER FIELD. SHE IS AN EXEMPLARY CITIZEN. This woman did not seem to be what Edith had in mind. She needed more than a good Samaritan to get her out of crisis. She needed a strict disciplinarian. Somebody compassionate, smart, but not too nice. Edith hated nice women.

The last degree confused her the most. The document testified that Alice Blakely had completed a course in T.A. So she was no longer a social worker, she was a Transactional Analyst. Edith noticed that she had only completed the course last year. Edith did not feel like being a guinea pig. She was afraid of experiments. The rats always ended up dead or with cancer.

The door in the waiting room opened. A pale white woman with greying blond hair walked in. A WASP, Edith choked. She should have known better. After all, how many Jewish therapists were there in Conway? How many Jews were there in New Hampshire? Edith Rebecca Greenblatt had not adequately prepared herself for talking to a gentile. On the phone these things never registered. She could never tell how white someone was on the phone.

Edith watched Alice Blakely hold her pale hand directly in front of Edith's waist, waiting for Edith's Jewish hand so they could shake together. Edith swallowed. She liked that the woman was clearly middle-aged; she had wanted to talk to an older woman. Edith shook Alice's hand with vigor. She wanted to let Alice know that she was totally committed to working with her.

"You must be Edith. I'm Alice Blakely. I hope you weren't waiting long."

"Hello." Edith was not going to mention that Alice's dog had accosted her. She did not want her new therapist to think she was afraid of animals. Edith followed Alice into her office. Alice Blakely's plump little body reminded Edith of her big sitting-up pillow.

"I can't sit too close to you. I'm just getting over a cold," Alice said, as she pushed her chair what seemed to be yards away from Edith. Alice didn't want to sit close to her clients, Edith thought, because she was afraid of catching depression. To Edith, the distance seemed more WASPy than anything else. When the Jews had a cold they all sat around blowing each other's noses. In fact, Edith had seen her own parents share the same square white handkerchief. But this was not the first time a WASP had had a cold and refused to sit next to her. Edith knew how to respond. She pushed her chair as far away from Alice's as possible, trying to show that she was sympathetic to the situation.

Once both women were seated, Edith looked around the room. It was more like a den or a playroom for kids than a counseling room. A huge playpen filled with stuffed animals was off to the left side of the sitting area. There was a blackboard on an easel near the couch. Colored chalk was in the tray with the erasers. Edith tried hard to get the feel of the room. But she was unable to get one single sensation. Alice sat up, blowing her nose. In a minute, Edith knew, her kleenex would be neatly returned to that place directly beneath Alice's watchband where women-with-colds tucked their hankies.

Alice sniffed. Edith looked for a cross around her neck. None. Good. She wouldn't be distracted. There was nothing worse than talking to a woman with a silver cross around her neck. Edith could never concentrate whenever she saw Christian jewelry. She always felt as though she were being converted.

"I'm depressed. I think I'm in crisis." Edith looked at Alice who was nodding her head with only her neck. Edith wondered if this was Alice's listening pose. The Jews listened with their whole bodies. They pushed their chairs in closer the more interesting the story became. They folded and unfolded their hands. Alice Blakely listened more with her head. Her entire body remained motionless. She looked as though she was sleeping with her eyes open.

"I feel self-destructive," Edith said. She saw Alice blink. "It's nothing to worry about. I'm used to the feeling by now. I can usually recognize it before I do anything drastic." Alice's mouth had opened several times and then closed immediately. Edith wasn't sure if she was gasping for breath or trying to interrupt with a good therapeutic question.

"That's not what I really want to talk about. I just wanted to give you some background. I've been unhappy for days. I can't seem to shake it." Edith had started talking with her hands.

"Could we get back to the self-destruction?" Alice was taking notes. Edith watched Alice underline the word *self-destruct*. She smiled to herself; it felt good to be taken seriously. She also liked talking about depression. Besides the Jews, it was — unfortunately — the one topic she knew a lot about.

"I've always thought if I was going to kill myself, I'd take rat poisoning. I remember learning in Hebrew school that the Jews of Warsaw carried cyanide tablets in small silver chains around their necks. When they couldn't defend themselves any longer they went down below the city to the sewers and swallowed the poison in private. They didn't want the army taking credit for their deaths. I want to die the same way."

"You're Jewish?" Alice said the word *Jewish* very loud. Edith sensed she didn't say the word often.

"Yes, I am a Jew. I like being a Jew. That has nothing to do with why I'm here." Every time Edith said *Jew* her voice got louder and louder. She wished Alice's cold would get worse so Alice would have to push her chair farther away.

"Why is it you want to kill yourself, Edith?" Good. She was being addressed by name.

"I'm unhappy. I barely go outside. I've been unhappy for months. I need you to help me." Alice was still writing furiously into her notebook.

"I've got to tell you what I'm thinking. I don't want to upset you or anything." Edith saw Alice put her pencil down. "It's okay that you're not a lesbian. I can handle that a whole lot better than the fact that you're not a Jew. I mean you are a woman." Edith was quiet for a few seconds. "Just what is your experience with Feminism? You ARE a FEMINIST aren't YOU?" Edith was trying to keep her voice flat. She did not want to upset Alice.

"Of course I am for equal rights and equal pay." Alice whispered. Her left hand was tucking her kleenex further under her watchband. "I do have a daughter, you know."

"What does that mean?" Edith had not come here to discuss politics. She hardly knew how they got onto women. Edith just wanted to talk. She could see herself sitting in front of her unplugged phone, watching the receiver, hoping the phone would ring anyway. She had to tell Alice about staring at her unplugged phone; about not letting any more *goyim* in.

"Well, it means that I support the liberation of women, for my daughter's sake." Alice coughed. "Do you always interview your therapist?" She glanced at her notes. "Now what were you saying?"

"JUDAISM." Edith bit her tongue so she wouldn't say anything else. She thought she was going to cry. Maybe she should apologize to Alice. But Alice was still looking at her notes. Edith couldn't seem to get her complete attention.

"I think I'm pretty upset about all this. What do you think?"

"What's this?"

"I forget that New England doesn't have a whole lot of Jews . . . there's mostly gentiles. Every time I . . . ."

"Mostly what?" Edith watched Alice write herself a

note in the margin of her notebook. Maybe she was reminding herself to look up more about the Jews.

"I'd like to get back to my depression. I don't want this Jewish thing to come between us. I'm used to being around gentiles." Edith was going to offer to spell *gentile* for Alice.

"Do you know much about Transactional Analysis?" Alice had bounced off her seat just like a high school cheerleader bouncing off the bleachers and onto the gym floor. Alice was standing next to the blackboard. She held the blue chalk in her hand. Edith had no idea why they were looking at the blackboard. She had not finished explaining her suffering. "In T.A. we divide the psyche into three parts." Alice was beaming. This was something she knew about. Edith stared at the three blue circles Alice drew on the board. Inside each circle she put a different letter of the alphabet. The first circle had a "C" then there was a "P" and an "A." Alice's head kept turning from the blackboard to Edith. She was making eye contact. "We in T.A. see the human being as though he were in constant struggle between the parent, adult, and child in himself."

Edith wanted to know *who was this we?* And was this divided psyche a Jewish or *goyisha* psyche? Edith had divided her own psyche quite a bit differently than the T.A. people. She wondered if she should interrupt Alice.

"The parent constantly corrects us. The parent constantly says SHOULD. We are most unhappy when the parent takes over. We feel forced to behave in ways we don't want to."

That sounded like the Jew in her. Edith was always telling herself that she should celebrate more holidays and eat less bacon and ham.

"The adult on the other hand . . ."

Alice seemed far away. Perhaps she had forgotten Edith was there, asking for help.

"The adult makes responsible choices based on his wants, needs and responsibilities within society at large."

Edith recognized that her adult-self was the lesbian in her. The most adult decision she had ever made was to come out of the closet.

"And the child always cries whenever he doesn't get his way, or whenever he feels totally misunderstood."

Alice wasn't exactly an artist. Her drawing was all stick figures, but obviously she had perfected her technique while in training. Edith was trying to figure out her child-self. Maybe the unhappy, depressed part of her was really the child, crying out for help. *That* was what she had wanted to talk about. Alice had returned to her seat. She looked pleased. She had not blown her nose once throughout the entire performance.

"Did that help you?"

"Well, to tell you the truth, I could have gotten the same idea if you had stayed in your seat. But it was helpful. I can see the child in me takes over a lot." Edith's own neck was stiff watching Alice's head go up and down. She seemed to agree with whatever Edith had to say. Evidently honesty was highly valued among the T.A. people. Edith wanted to scream; why didn't Alice Blakely tell her to be quiet and listen. Somebody had to be willing to tell Edith that she didn't know everything.

"I think your problem is with the child in you." Immediately Edith sat up and decided not to scream. "In T.A. we try to isolate that part of the psyche which is suffering the most."

"Do you think you could stop saying in *T.A. we* ... I mean, I'm just not sure who is talking to me. I like to think you can make your own conclusions about my life." Edith wondered if she'd gone too far; she felt the child in her was taking over.

"I'm not sure what you mean, but I can see you are in pain."

"I really don't want to tell you how to run this session, but I stop listening as soon as you say those words." Edith tried to smile at her new therapist, but Alice was staring hard at her client as if she was trying to make her disappear.

"You see, I was right. The child in you is most unhappy. I'm sorry if my method offends you." Edith wanted to lift Alice Blakely's round little body off its gentile seat and shake it up and down until the woman yelled at Edith to shut up. Alice just sat there staring hard and cold at her. She was absolutely the most unreachable human being Edith had ever met in her entire life. Edith felt herself withdrawing. In fact she wanted to stand up and run out to her car, but she was afraid the German Shepherd would get her. Edith decided to be a good client. She put her hands together and then placed them directly into her lap.

"I have been depressed my whole life. Lately it's getting worse. Can you help me?"

"Do your parents know you're a lesbian?"

"What?"

"Your parents, your mother . . ."

"Oh no, of course not." Edith had decided long ago never to tell her parents unless they asked first. Jews tended to see all things they didn't understand as tragic. Edith knew that having a grandmother who survived Auschwitz and having a lesbian in the same family were incompatible if your parents were Jews.

"What I think I am really upset about is my depression." Edith said it louder. "I'm depressed."

"It seems to me your mother would want to know that you have found someone to share your life with . . ."

"I do not want to tell my parents. They wouldn't understand. Besides I like coming home for Rosh Hashonah and the Seder.

"Seder?"

"Passover."

"Oh, yes, that's like our Last Supper, isn't it? About the child in you, Edith, you seem so unhappy. Worse now than when you came in. It just seemed to make sense, that if your mother knew about you and a . . ."

"Schwartzie."

"Schwartzie, you would be a lot happier. Do you enjoy yourself much?" Alice had stopped taking notes.

"Actually, I can't remember the last time I was really happy. It seems to me I have always been sad." Edith wanted to curl up in a little ball. She hated reminding herself how unhappy she was. There had never been anyone who could help her. She wanted to ask Alice if she understood about her parents, but that didn't seem to be the issue anymore.

"Can you remember specifics?"

"There's not a whole lot to tell. I just seem to be unhappy all the time. I don't know why."

"It is clear. You do not enjoy yourself."

"Yes." Edith already knew that.

"Do you think being a Jew has made you unable to have fun?"

"What does being Jewish have to do with not being able to have fun?"

"In T.A. we like to go back to the beginning, you know Genesis. We feel it's important to understand our roots."

"I already understand where I come from. This is absolutely not helping me."

"I'm sorry you feel that way. I think you are resisting. I have seen this kind of reaction before. Your kind always think you're right." Edith saw that Alice was determined to counsel her.

"I'd like you to get in this playpen." Alice was

schlepping the thing over to Edith's chair. "I want you to get inside and play with the animals."

Edith had never done anything like this before. She decided to go along with Alice. Nothing could make her feel worse than she felt now. Besides, maybe Alice did know what she was doing; maybe Edith would be happier after she got inside the playpen. She got up from her chair and lifted her right leg up so high she almost fell over the top bar. Jumping off the ground slightly, she was able to put her foot evenly down on the pegboard floor. One more jump and she was inside waiting for her next set of instructions.

"Good girl. How do you feel?" Alice was clearly happy. Everything was back the way the T.A. people said it should be.

Edith tried to get comfortable. The bottom of the playpen was hard. She could see why children never stayed inside for long. She was uncomfortable herself. But for the sake of becoming a happy person, she would try to cooperate.

"Pick up your favorite animal and talk to it. Tell it everything you always wanted to say as a child, but kept buried inside yourself instead. We in T.A. do this all the time. We call it *reconnecting*." Alice was almost singing. She had a lovely little *shiksa* voice. Edith could just see Alice dressed in a purple choir robe, singing about Jesus Christ and smiling one big grin. Edith wanted to ask her to stop saying the T.A. slogan, but it didn't seem worth the effort. Instead she looked around for her favorite animal. As a child she had played nonstop with a small tan fox. "I really don't have a favorite, Alice. None of these is my kind."

"Can't you just pick one? I like the giraffe myself. Try the giraffe. Go on pick it up, Edith."

"Alright." The giraffe was cute. His head was about six inches from his body. That reminded Edith of herself. Lots of times she felt like her Jewish body and her Jewish mind were miles apart. Edith liked the brown spots on the giraffe. "This isn't working." She put down the stuffed giraffe and looked through the bars for Alice's face.

"What do you mean, this isn't working? Of course it is." Alice was taking notes.

"I'm not happy. I don't feel anything."

"You're not supposed to feel or think. You're supposed to talk to that giraffe so I can observe you. Now start TALKING." Alice didn't look up from her notebook; she was too busy writing. Edith could almost feel the word *RESISTING* coming out of her pencil as she wrote. Edith felt ridiculous. What was a twenty-six-year-old Jewish lesbian doing on the floor of her *goyisha* therapist's playpen?" Edith stood up; she dragged her right leg over the top bar.

"What are you doing?" Alice had finally looked up from her notebook. She walked over to Edith. "Don't you understand, you have to stay in there. It's for your own good." Alice tried to push Edith back inside. She put her hands on Edith's shoulders. Edith was sure Alice wasn't very strong. Edith counted to three. She collected her strength. She sucked in all the air she could and then heaved straight up. Alice fell back. For a moment both women were completely still. Edith felt herself taking over the session, but that was not what she wanted at all. She didn't know what to do with herself. Alice walked slowly back towards the playpen; she straightened her hair. Edith could feel her thinking. If Alice tried to touch her again, Edith knew she would jump up and lash out at the woman. Edith had been listening for too long. She was exhausted. All she wanted was to be held, to have her head massaged gently so she could sleep. Alice wasn't going to let her sleep. Edith saw it in her eyes. Alice's hands were on top of the playpen. She leaned over, bending her head inside the cage. She put her face as close to Edith's face as she possibly could without touching her. In a very loud voice she said,

"GET OUT. You are obviously resisting treatment, so get out." Alice took her head out of the playpen and looked at her watch.

Edith couldn't talk. She didn't know if she was supposed to get out of Alice's house or just get out of her playpen. She couldn't believe she had almost tried to beat up her therapist. She didn't think she could ever tell anyone. Who would believe her? She thought she wanted to laugh, but she never laughed when she was depressed.

"We have to end now. We've already gone over our time limit. I am going to ask you to do one more thing — not for me — for yourself, Edith. It's up to you, of course."

"Yes?" Edith hated favors.

"I want you to be depressed for fifteen minutes every day until your next appointment. I want you to sit in your room, or wherever you get depressed the best. Keep telling yourself how horrible you feel, think about being Jewish, and then see if you can cry a little. Write it all down and we'll talk about it." Edith nodded.

"I hope I have helped you. Your kind of depression is quite severe. Why don't you come again on Monday?"

That was only three days away. It seemed too soon. Edith wasn't sure that she ever wanted to see this woman again. "Yes, that's great." Why was she agreeing to come back? Why couldn't she say *no*? "What time?"

"Three o'clock."

Edith stood up.

"Do you want a hug?" Edith didn't believe what she just heard. She turned towards the door. Alice stood in front of her with her arms stretched out, ready to embrace Edith with the whole of her Christian body. Edith thought maybe this was a trick, and that if she hugged Alice back, her therapist was really going to try and hit her or force her back into the playpen. Edith stared hard at Alice. She was wrong. The end here where Alice gets to offer her client a hug, was her favorite part. That's what she must be known for. HUGGY ALICE BLAKELY. No matter how the session went, she always hopped up in the end, waiting to take her client into her breast. Edith shuddered. That was one breast she could live without.

"No, thank you."

"Oh, I should have known, you're not the hugging type. I can see it now." Alice looked relieved. She reunited her arms with the rest of her body. She had probably never hugged a Jewish lesbian before and didn't know exactly what to do. They shook hands instead.

On her way to the car, Edith told herself to plug her phone back in as soon as she got home. First she would call Alice Blakely and cancel their Monday appointment. Then she'd call Schwartzie and tell her The Depression was beginning to lift.

Such a Business

MARCY ALANCRAIG

1931

"VEY IZ MIR," Rheabie muttered, rushing to meet Mae Cherney, her nearest neighbor, from the hollow center of a Monday afternoon. "May it be quick, this chat. Then enough, thanks for the memories, goodbye." She didn't like what she had to say to the fiery woman but better the words spoken than held in her mouth, heavy as stones. "To tangle with such a temper! For a woman my age this kind of foolishness should be over already, done." She shook her head, hurrying to their regular meeting place, an outcropping of rock that glowered from the hill above their chicken ranches. The Northern California slope clutched at her calves as she climbed.

"So what's the rush?" Mae smiled down from her familiar perch with welcoming eyes. "You've got a train to catch, maybe?"

"No. Something to say." Rheabie felt the walk suddenly: staccato drumbeats throbbing her wrists, lungs flushed to a burn. She steadied herself with a look at all the farms stretching east in a litter of chicken sheds to downtown

Petaluma. "Egg basket of the world," the merchants bragged. The horror of that basket, it should ever know what she and Mae had done.

Rheabie took a breath. "It is against my principles, Mae Cherney, what happened last night. Never again, such a wrongful act. Of this in our friendship I cannot approve."

"Be ashamed!" Mae roared. She scrambled down the rock and shook Rheabie's shoulders. "A crime you should lie to me!"

"I'm not."

"You are. Some kind of 'wrongful act,' Missus Truthteller — you didn't want it to end!" Mae let her go and folded her arms. "Tell me how a kiss — in the dark, the back of a truck yet — it offends principles?"

"With our husbands up front, any minute they could turn around?" A mishegoss under the eyes of the stars. Rheabie had watched the glittering lights for most of the ride home last night from the Petaluma Jewish Center. The quiet eased the heat of the hall from her body, swept the clamor of the monthly gathering away. All evening she'd heard opinions about eggs and the Soviet Union from nearly every Jewish rancher in the county. Afterwards she'd preferred the back of the windblown Ford to another second of doctrinaire noise. Especially from those czars of dialectics, her Jake, and Mae's Art.

"Phui! So busy ridiculing the Zionist position, those two, who would see? Stalin should be grateful. They shovel chicken shit all day *and* solve the leader's problems. If only he'd listen, Comrade Joseph. The man could live a life of ease!"

Rheabie held back her smile. Last night, just such a comment had startled her into laughter. The glad wheeze had sparked the moonlight, a shower of sound that winked with the Milky Way. She'd caught her breath between chuckles and turned to the joker beside her. What made her pat the nearby

72

lips with a trembling finger? Or cup the freckled neck so that Mae's grin brushed hers? A hesitant touch flared into hunger. Rheabie cringed at the memory. She'd opened her mouth and tasted half the sky.

She drew the April breeze in against her teeth and spoke quietly. "In the truck, Mae, more than the touch of friends. I am a married woman. I have family, a peace to make in my home."

Hurt bleached her neighbor's face. "And my barrenness makes me different?" Then she snorted. "Of course. I forgot. Comrade Rheabie, the wedded slave." Mae narrowed her eyes. "You call yourself a socialist? What kind of peace do you make from a ceremony, a bourgeois convention? Emma Goldman should hear your words and spit."

Rheabie straightened. "*I* spit on a *meshuggeneh* anarchist." Her hands gripped anger: it never ended, the Cherney nerve! To take a position on their embrace, state a politics — as if the simple fact of Mae's mouth on hers, a softness that warmed the night, couldn't be wrong. "Feh! You and your nonsense, this free love!"

Besides, what did Mae know from such a business? A woman who ignited each time Art bedded another emancipated female. The free-thinker who watched her husband with knives in her eyes.

Those knives had never edged toward Rheabie during the two crowded years they'd been neighbors to each other. Intelligence and sympathy always laced the woman's gaze. And, truth be told, it was Mae's glint that had driven the memory of Rheabie's mother back to her reluctant grave in Terlitza. When the haunting ended, it was Comrade Cherney whose wide vision wove the old country memories, Ukrainian songs and Mama's sorrows, into a scarf of peace.

This she planned to give up — the green-eyes woman, her transforming laughter — because of kissing? All right, the kissing. But could she bear to go back to the long loneliness of

73

her days before Mae?

Yes, of course. If she had to. If it took away the danger. Because, she swore on her mother's brave and short life, this thing between them that could hurt her family — never again.

Rheabie turned and found herself looking down, searching for Jake among the buildings that nestled into the hill below them. She wanted to wave to him: a slumped figure recounting the day's take in the door of the egg shed, the worry of the mortgage weighing his back. Had he found the cake she'd left as a surprise on the kitchen table? Would he share it with the young ones or snarl when they stumbled in, hungry, after school?

"Listen!" Mae blocked her view. "I know the truth of your life, Rheabie Slominski. Since the Crash the *shlemiel* you share your bed with is different, an angry man. Blind to you and the *kinder*. Not smart enough to see past the fear in his eyes. But I see, missus. I am the only one who cares you should need."

Rheabie fought a rush of tears. "A plague on your words. So all right, Jake is a bear with his worries. It's a crime he doesn't want we should be foreclosed?"

"Yes." Mae insisted. She lifted Rheabie's chin. "A crime to make misery for everyone out of a worry. To chase happiness from the house with his thick hands. Even with the state of the egg market, we are allowed to smile, *bubeleh*. A little pleasure we get in this wretched thing called life."

"Pleasure doesn't make a better world, hold a family. What are you doing? You want I should leave my responsibilities?"

Mae placed a hand on Rheabie's cheek. "Dear heart, stop." She blotted the path of a tear. "We are agreed, yes, on the woman question? You're forgetting our position. Thinking small."

"I'm not," she cried, feeling the lash of Jake's daily

curses bruising her back, remembering Mae's kiss, warm as a summer plum. "This is life we're talking, not positions. My husband. *My* family." She crouched by the rock and sobbed.

Rheabie felt herself gathered up in strong arms. "Sha. It's all right, dolly. What's a position if it's only talk? Between us here, something to live!"

"No." The truth walled her throat. She stumbled on the granite words. "Emma Goldman, her free love, even she didn't mean this — a woman and a woman."

Mae held her closer. "*Nu,*" she shrugged. "Who makes the law, how love has to be?"

Rheabie drew back to stare at a stranger. "But a woman and a woman..." Mae returned her look without blinking. Her eyes took the shape of trees. Cheeks widened into meadows. Rheabie saw plowed fields in the place of braided hair. She shook her head and spoke to the unknown landscape. "What is this? A whole new country you want I should go."

Mae smiled. "You're telling me from Terlitza to California was some kind of small journey?"

"No." She remembered night skies laced with grief, weeping over Mama's murder. Days without words, inhaling the scent of fear. Would she escape the army that had killed her entire family? Did the woman, her guide, know enough to dodge the hungry patrols?"

"*Bubee,* I've done this," Mae whispered.

The exhilaration of crossing the border, achieving passage in Bremen. Walking the belly of the boat. Looking forward, finally, into the sea.

"From this voyage," Mae crooned, "nothing you should be afraid."

Rheabie drew the new land down beside her. She kissed the soil that pressed against her limbs. The river bed of Mae's mouth tasted of sunlight. April breezes fluttered from the palms of her hands.

The two women nestled in the shadow of the great rock and wove themselves into an embrace of grasses. Rheabie gurgled surprise at the pleasures of earth, skin grazing skin.

"Soft," she breathed: the slope of a thigh, steppe of belly. "Sweet, so soft." Land flooded the narrow cage of her bones.

She stretched, becoming hillside, becoming grasses. "Such a business," Rheabie panted, the continent's pulse rushing her blood. "Mae," she called, growing big enough to devour the horizon. "*Ai yi yi,* my Maedela." She swallowed galaxies, inhaled a stream of suns.

"*Oh vey,* that was something."

A lark song beat in Rheabie's throat. She opened her eyes to the flurry of wings. The bird hovered near them for a moment, caught an air current and lifted away. "Such a pleasure," she smiled to Mae.

"The bird or me?"

Rheabie laughed. She sat up and grabbed a stalk of wild mustard. "You," she promised, dribbling the blooms across Mae's chest. The yellow petals caught the edge of afternoon sunlight. Rheabie touched them gently, then bent to chase their stains with her tongue.

"Immigrant," Mae breathed. "Not a greenhorn, you, the customs of this 'woman-and-woman' country. Did you catch on so quick before, my Ellis Island girl?"

The earth still sounded in her body. Rheabie's eyes teared with the slow joy that tattooed her skin. "Some kind of miracle, yes? Last night, today—all I felt was frightened. But for the pleasure of you," she said, "I have wandered into a place, like Petaluma, I will make some kind of home."

Excerpted from *Hatching Ground: A Novel of Petaluma*

My
Grandmother's Plates

ELANA DYKEWOMON

FIFTEEN YEARS after my grandmother died, my aunt Glory sends me a box with my grandmother's glass plates and matching goblets. A note precedes them. "Your mother and I thought you should have something material that belonged to Rose. I have used them for years — they're a very handy size for salads and lunch."

A week later I am carrying the box home from the post office. I set it on the couch and hold my breath. I remember the carpet in my grandmother's dining room, the newspapers over the carpet, the heavy wood sideboards, a needlepoint replica of the unicorn tapestries that one of my grandmother's sisters made. I loved my grandmother, and she loved me. I was never very attached to the rest of my family. After she died, I moved farther north, then far west.

My grandmother kept kosher on the eighth floor of West End & 86th Street in New York City. I had a key. When she traveled, visiting her daughters, I'd bring my high school friends in to smoke dope, make love, sit naked on her furniture — but I never let them touch the dishes. I only let them eat take-out on paper plates. Grandma, I'd say, don't worry, you can trust me, I never mix the meat & milk, I never let anyone into the cupboards.

Now I open the box not knowing what to expect. A heavy, square goblet appears, alternating panels and circles of clear and rose. The plate matches. Yes, I think, a handy size, a little bigger than salad but not a full dinner plate. I can only take out one glass, one dish. I leave them there, on the couch. I don't write my aunt (don't bother, she said, I know how busy you are, that's why I got a return receipt). Do I recognize them, are they ghosts?

Fifteen years later I'm 39 — why did they decide to send these to me? After finally visiting my home did they decide I was too poor, would never have wedding presents? Or did I become real somehow and now they want to reconnect me to them, to tradition? Are these meat or milk dishes? Were they everyday or for Pesach? I think I remember them but what I remember is the crackers in the oven, the tiny kitchen, the matzah meal in the closet above the ironing board, the smell of chicken soup in the hallway.

My aunt, who keeps kosher still, sent these between Purim and Pesach. Maybe it was just spring cleaning, and she held a feather in her hand — some *chumetz* in a corner — something she thought she owed me or something else that needed new space — clear these out, send them away. I question my mother in the mail, and her answer is sweet, but the same: we were thinking you didn't have anything from your grandmother, and we wanted you to have these.

I have grandmother's menorah, and a few little things I took when she died. But those are what I took, not what they gave. Maybe they both feel guilty I didn't get the writing desk I'd asked for; maybe it's the way women express their fear of mortality — handing down their rings, their plates. We will be alright, everything will go well with us if you don't break the dishes, if you carry them with you when you move, if you send them to your nieces when you have some — unbroken dishes down three generations means extraordinary luck, for Jews, no pogroms, no forced evacuations.

I keep the open, unpacked box on my couch for two weeks until I have a lesbian meeting in the house and have to move them to the back porch. I feel I cannot use them until I've koshered them somehow, changed them from kosher to mine. Performed some ritual that keeps faith with the faith of the women who've gone before me. Something instinctual, female, that has nothing to do with intellectual belief.

How do you kosher dishes? I ask my friends. They say you take them to the ocean and dip them in salt water. Ocean water koshers objects. Of course this ritual has been changed to salt water in the kitchen and a couple prayers. Or, they say, you *could* take them to the mikvah. I'm not sure this is true but I develop an elaborate fantasy of carrying these glass plates into the San Francisco mikvah.

I've never been to a mikvah, I don't know if my mother has ever been to a mikvah, certainly she's never spoken about one. A mikvah is a ritual bath, where women go after menstruating, to make themselves "clean" again. I've seen one in the Jewish movies, something about being immersed in the water, a dunking and turning.

In my mind it's an ancient cave, tile protruding from limestone ledges, fed by an underground passage to the sea, heated dangerously, mysteriously. I imagine small groups of orthodox women dropping their towels, letting their real hair fall around their necks, stepping carefully down the slippery limestone steps.

Into this steamy yellow cave I carry my brown box full of clear and rose glass plates. I put the box on the side of the pool and first immerse myself in whatever ritual is given me by the woman attending the bath. Naked, I pull the dishes and goblets out one by one, dunk them in the mikvah, wrap them in clean towels, place them back in the box while the orthodox women watch, smiling at me.

The dishes sit on my back porch. Eventually I write my aunt a thank-you note. I don't lug them to the Pacific, I don't find the mikvah. Every now and then I think about it, tripping on the box while opening or closing the back porch window. Lag b'Omer, Shavous, Tish b'Av go by without notice.

Then, on the second day of Rosh Hashona, I invite my friend Sophie over for breakfast — bagels, whitefish salad, lox, avocado, onion, tomato, cream cheese. I go to the cupboard to get plates and stop still. Oh, I say, it's the new year, I know what we'll use.

Two plates come out of the box. It's that simple. Sophie, who's my neighbor and dear friend, listens to my story about the plates and the mikvah, but concentrates on the lox. We enjoy our new year's feast.

The plates — seem very pretty. Almost too pretty to be mine. Two plates in the dishdrainer, in the stack in the cupboard. All the others, and the goblets, stay on the porch. I am very careful with these two dishes, I only eat fish and dairy on them, never meat.

I used to say my family never gave me anything, not anything from the heart.

The
Cart O'Tea Belove

MARTHA SHELLEY

THE PHONE RANG, a clangor that mangled her nerves and set her heart racing. Nikki opened an eye. Clock hands wavered, luminescent fronds in a murky sea.

Ilana grabbed the receiver. "Hi, *Ima!*" she said, and then rattled away cheerfully in Hebrew while Nikki pulled the pillow over her head. Useless, unless she smothered herself completely.

"Why does your mom always call at four a.m.?" Nikki groaned.

"*Sheket!*" Ilana whispered fiercely, putting a hand over the mouthpiece and continuing as though she hadn't been interrupted. Finally she hung up and Nikki tried to soothe herself back into unconsciousness, but just as she was drifting off she heard a thump from the children's room and Yoav was out of his crib, through the door, kicking a space for himself between them. "Monster," Nikki whispered, trailing her finger along the delicate coil of his ear. He brushed it away, instantly sinking into the sleep denied to her.

A good time to draw him. When she first met Ilana she

constantly drew the kids, stills in the bedroom, furious sketches in the playground, but now the thought of getting up to hunt for a pad exhausted her, and hadn't the kids torn the last one up for paper airplanes? Then it was half past five and dawn was streaming through the bedroom window.

Nikki stumbled into the kitchen, filled the kettle, shut the faucet with a vicious twist. Now she'd have to drink coffee to make it through the day, the cycle beginning again, caffeine to wake, dope to sleep, the whole thing ending with migraines that lasted for days.

"Doesn't she remember what it's like to have kids?" Nikki grumbled. "Or is this your mother's idea of revenge?"

"Americans are so damn spoiled," Ilana shot back. "It costs ten times more calling out from Israel than calling in. She has to wait till the rates are low."

Mrs. Katinsky phoned every month and it always provoked the same argument. But today Ilana added, "She's coming in July."

"What?"

"Are you getting deaf? I told you, my mother is coming."

Nikki winced. Well, I asked for it, she told herself.

The summer before, Ilana's in-laws had come to America to console their only son, condemn his faithless wife and see what Berkeley perversion she was teaching the children. Then Mrs. K. called to complain that Zalman's parents were spreading a scandal. "Why don't you come and see for yourself?" Ilana said, and in a moment of pride or reckless generosity, Nikki encouraged Ilana to invite her. "Let her see we're not so awful. The kids are healthy, you're happy. I'm not a slimeball from the bottom of the Bay." So Ilana wrote her mother a four-page letter. Mrs. Katinsky bought a ticket.

Nikki counted out three oranges apiece, bisected them and whirled them through the juicer. There's now way out, she thought. Aloud, she said, "How long is she going to stay?"

82

"A month."

"A month! I can hardly stand my own parents more'n four days at a time."

Yoav climbed into a chair and banged his plastic cup against the table. "Owanj juice," he said. "Want owanj juice."

"Nikki, be reasonable. A woman her age isn't schlepping halfway around the world for a four-day weekend."

"Mom, should I wear the pink blouse or the yellow?" Tali was the middle child in more ways than one, neither dark like Ilana nor blond like her father, with fawn-colored eyes and hair.

"Whatever you like, Talika. No, wear the yellow. The pink one's dirty."

"But the pink one has ducks on it."

"Owanj juice!"

Nikki filled the cup. "Where are we going to put her?" They had two bedrooms, a bath, and an L-shaped affair that served as livingroom and kitchen, with a dinette set at the junction.

"In our bed. We'll sleep in the living room."

"No." Nikki moved firmly to squash that idea. "It's bad enough with the kids barging in." As it was she had to fight for every private moment. She nagged Ilana to make Zalman pick up the kids on time so they could catch a movie, she bullied Shimon into bed at ten so the women could have an hour together before they collapsed from exhaustion. It'll only be worse if we lived in Israel, she thought, without Zalman babysitting twice a month.

"Maybe I'll put her in Shimon's bed."

"Put who? You're not putting no girls in my bed." At the sound of his name, the first-born dragged himself into the kitchen. He was the owl, his brother the lark.

"Cheewios," Yoav said, grasping the cereal box with both hands and pouring little brown circles into his bowl. They formed a conical heap, spilling over onto the tablecloth with a pleasant rustle.

"Your grandmother's coming."

"Oh, she's not a girl. Well, she is but you know what I mean. I'll let her have my bed if I get to sleep on the couch and stay up late and watch any program I want."

"She can sleep in my bed," Tali said. "Can I have a sunshine egg?"

"Sunnyside up," Nikki said.

"This place is a horrible mess, just horrible," Ilana said. "I'll have to take off Friday and clean it."

"Oh god, not again," Nikki said.

"Believe me, it won't be like last year," Ilana promised. "My mother's not as fanatic as Zalman's mother."

Yoav shook the last Cheerio out of the box. He stared at the pile intently. Then, with a series of energetic swipes, he knocked the excess to the floor. "Now want milk," he said.

Last year a similar announcement preceded the arrival of Zalman's parents. Nikki had been mopping the floor, meditating on the dirt that could accumulate in two days' time. If they didn't mop every other day she imagined a midden would develop, a congealed layer of jam and bread crumbs, peanut butter and crushed Cheerios. The apartment sat smack at ground level, and unless they locked the windows the kids climbed in and out all day — so much more fun than using the door — and the neighborhood kids came with them, drizzling raisins and ice cream and brightly colored plastic wheels. She fantasized some future archeologist writing a paper on the dietary habits of late 20th century Californians, and what would they make of the plastic wheels?

Just then Ilana came home, Yoav on one hip and a bag of groceries on the other. "This is a disgusting mess," she said.

"Are you crazy? I just finished cleaning."

"It's encrusted with dirt. Zalman's parents are coming

next week. I'll just have to take off from work to clean up."

"We mop three times a week," Nikki said. "When I lived alone I mopped the floor three, maybe four times a year."

"Whether it needed it or not," Ilana retorted. "Look, Zalman's father tried to make him take the kids away from me. He said if Zalman can't raise them himself, it's better to put them in an orphanage than leave them with lesbians. And if they see us living in a pigsty . . . ."

"Who cares what they think? Zalman doesn't want custody, so what can they do?"

"Here, nothing. But I don't want trouble from them in Israel."

"So why are you always talking about moving there? It's so much easier to raise them here."

"What am I going to do here? Who needs another Ph.D. in Berkeley? Look, I just got a letter from Tel-Aviv. There's a job waiting for me, I just have to finish the dissertation. Nu, it's not your problem. I'll clean it myself."

It's not your problem, the tape began, and the rest of it played silently in Nikki's head. They're not your kids. You can come and go as you please. No matter how much she did she could never earn parental rights to the children she'd come to love, never compete financially with Zalman the accountant. But the louder the tape played the more she rolled her boulder uphill, and as the week progressed she found herself taking curtains down to be laundered, washing windows and scrubbing crayon marks off the walls.

"How long are they going to stay?" Nikki asked.

"A month."

"That's crazy! We can't put them up for a month."

"*Bulbul,* they're staying with Zalman. But I have to invite them for dinner. They want to see how their grandchildren live."

"All this, just for one dinner?"

As the time drew near, Ilana got frantic. Nikki came home from work on Friday and found her down on her knees scraping yellow goo from the corners around the stove.

"Who's gonna notice that?" Nikki said.

"Believe me, Zalman's mother will." Ilana pushed a stray hair out of her eyes and stood up. "I need a break," she said, putting water on the stove.

When they were sitting at the table she said, "Nikkileh, this is really nothing. You can't imagine what it was like when I first got married. One week my parents would come, the next week Zalman's. Every Thursday night the cleaning would start. I'd be working like a donkey and Zalman would supervise and complain. It had to be perfect, just like his mother's house, otherwise you knew she'd be telling all her friends that her son married a *zhlub*." She took Nikki's hand in hers and caressed it. "I can't believe I stood it for so long. You don't know what a miracle you made in my life."

Nikki laughed. "My grandmother was like that. She used to say her house was so clean, you could eat from the toilet."

"That's Zalman's mother exactly. Her very words."

They gazed at each other for a long time, each perhaps thinking the same thing. They both had hair the color of black coffee, thick and loosely curled, they had the same dark eyes, wide hips and small hands. They could have been cousins in the old country, but Nikki's parents fled to New York after the first big war. Ilana's came after the second, to Jerusalem.

Nikki felt the silk of her lover's fingers and thought, Once she's through with school she'll see how ridiculous this is. We'll never make it as a couple over there.

Ilana gulped down the last of her coffee. "Let's finish before the kids come home," she said.

Nikki went in the bathroom and sprayed everything with Fantastik. She thought the chemicals were worse than dirt, but you couldn't argue with the older generation, and anyway this was a lot faster than soap and a scrub brush. *"Schmutz raus,"* she whispered morbidly in German, then turned on the shower and watched the suds spiral down, thinking of the fish at the other end of the drain and then of New York and Jerusalem. While she'd been dancing in lesbian bars, Ilana was learning to take an Uzi apart. When Nikki marched with the gay revolution, Ilana got married and bore Shimon.

There's a difference between those who escaped before the '40s, she thought, and the Survivors. But even her own family left relatives behind who didn't make it, and that tribal legacy hung over them both like a poisonous cloud.

She wiped toothpaste off the mirror and hair out of the soap dish and scrubbed the toilet till it shone. Then she balanced a fork on one side of the seat, a knife and spoon on the other.

"Hey, Ilana," she called. "Come look."

Ilana poked her head around the corner. "What . . . ?"

"Conceptual art. Your in-laws want to eat in here, it's ready."

"I'm sure they'll appreciate it," she laughed. She draped an arm across Nikki's shoulder and Nikki drank in the warmth, the feline sweat-smell that made her hunger for this woman.

She'd been planning to take a part-time job and enjoy the summer, go camping, do some painting. Visions tugged at her: eucalyptus trees on a ridge, the shimmery light on their leaves that made her stoned to look at it, wind-blown patterns in the golden grass beneath them. A stream descending, the first rills cascading smooth as muscle and foaming on the rocks below, each drop exploding with light, the light that she wanted to capture, that somehow kept receding. Anyway, how could she paint with Mrs. K. around?

Like having her own mother come. A painter? What kind of job is that? You'll starve. You'll go crazy and cut off your ear.

Nikki picked up the phone. "Hey Jeff," she said when her call went through, "you think Variola Inc. needs a summer typist?"

"I could ask," he said. "One of the other girls just quit. Same as last year, three days a week?"

"No, full-time. I'm out of school till September. And I gotta get out of the house."

He put her on hold and came back almost immediately. "Can you start tomorrow?"

"You bet!" She set the receiver down and sighed. Variola Inc. wasn't a bad place to work. She didn't like Mr. Valdt, the boss; if she came too close, she could hear the disk drive humming under his three-piece suit. But she got along with the office manager, a pleasant if rather conservative kid straight out of business school. And she'd made friends with Jeff, a WASPish guy who collected bad jokes and tried to understand the women's movement. He knew she was gay right off. The work was mindless, not too stressful. Most of all, it would be a legitimate refuge from family life, a real job, not something a mother could dismiss as egotistical indulgence.

Vaguely, she wondered when she would get to paint again.

The year before, when Zalman's parents came to dinner, Nikki decided to bake a pie to show them that dykes could cook too. She took Shimon along to pick blackberries. They'd found a jungle of vines in an empty lot next to a body shop.

"Are you sure it's okay to take their berries?" Shimon asked. He was blond and cautious, like his father.

"Let's ask." Just as she figured, the mechanics winked and asked if she'd make an extra pie for them, and she smiled and said maybe next time. Then she waded into the brambles.

"See? Use a glove to hold the canes and pick berries with the naked hand."

"The thorns are going through my pants," Shimon said, popping a berry into his mouth.

"Just pull them away slowly."

It was one of the few things they shared, this love of the outdoors. In so many other ways he was his father's son, clean and organized, concerned with appearances. According to Ilana, Zalman's parents were delighted with their first grandchild. "He looks just like a young lord," they crowed.

"That means he doesn't look Jewish," Ilana explained, making a wry face.

And neither did Zalman, Nikki thought. Maybe his blond hair saved him. But all she knew of those days was the story Ilana had told her, how Zalman's parents fled into Russia with their infant son. The baby had sick lungs, and there was nothing to eat. Then somehow they got hold of an orange, and they squeezed it drop by drop into a spoon and fed it to him, and he lived.

Shimon interrupted her reverie. "You ever meet my grandparents?" he asked.

"No."

"I did, mmf, when I was in Israel, mmf, last year." His lips dripped purple, his hands were crimson with crushed fruit.

"Hey, save some for the pie! What are they like?"

"Sweet."

"Your grandparents?"

"No, the berries. My grandparents are strict. Do you think they'll like you?"

"I doubt it."

"Then why are you making them pie?"

"I don't know."

When they finally arrived, Nikki was mildly surprised to see a stoop-shouldered old couple, almost a little fragile. Well, dummy, she told herself. What did you expect? Mr. and Mrs. Dracula? Zalman's mother was polite but the father turned away when Nikki was introduced. "What do you want?" Ilana said later. "You ran off with me and humiliated his son. Should he shake your hand?"

For dinner they had Ilana's borscht with sour cream and thick slices of rye. They spoke rapid-fire Hebrew, which was just as incomprehensible to Nikki as English was to them, so she contented herself with ladling out the soup and keeping the kids in line. Then she served them pie and coffee and finally Zalman came by to pick them up. The visit was over, almost as soon as it had begun.

"Condescending bitch!" Ilana said after they'd gone. "You know what she said about you? 'Ilana, my dear, it seems you've acquired a nice little helper.'"

"What nerve! Just where does she get off . . . ?"

"They didn't come to Israel to build a socialist state," Ilana said contemptuously. "All they ever wanted was to be Polish aristocrats."

"Too bad they finished the pie," Shimon said, scooping up a handful of crumbs.

Just as Ilana promised, the cleaning was easier this time, but Nikki was more apprehensive. Last year they'd been on the same team, with Zalman's parents as the opposition. Now Nikki felt the rules had changed. She found herself whining, "It's really gonna be hard, having a guest here for a month."

"She's not a guest, she's my mother. And if it gets too hard, you can always go to your studio."

You mean cop out, Nikki thought, and the guilt rose up

in her throat. She tried to be a partner and co-parent but she could never match Ilana, rising at six to get the kids dressed and out, teaching all morning and spending her afternoons in the library or the child care center, then shopping and cooking and working on her thesis till midnight or one the following morning. These sabras never complain, Nikki told herself. They just go until they drop.

She had to admit their relationship had changed over the last year, too. The first year she was high all the time, bursting with the newness of falling in love with four people at once, taking photos, taking them camping, painting their faces for Purim and Halloween. She told herself the divorce would soon be over, Yoav would learn to sleep through the night, she'd finish her degree and get a part-time teaching job. Then she'd have time for her art again.

But the struggle with Zalman dragged on. The kids were always up too late or up too early, and she'd start with one cup of coffee and the next day she'd need two, then three, and then a joint to calm down. Then, especially before her period, the headaches would come, like a piton driven in her skull and twisted, day after day. She found herself screaming at Ilana.

"I can't stand it anymore! I can't be a painter and a parent. If it goes on one more day, I'm gonna drive out to the bridge and jump!"

"It's my fault," Ilana replied in a shaky voice. "I'm making you suffer. You'd be better off if you left us."

"No, no! I just want to have more time with you. Zalman went on vacation, why can't you get him to take the kids for a week so we can go?"

"You know he won't do it. You need time off, why don't you go camping with your friends?"

"Dammit, don't you even want to go with me?"

"Want? What does what I want have to do with it? I give you everything I have to give. The kids come first, then you, and me last."

"No, then your dissertation, and your family, and me last!" Nikki shrieked.

"What do you want me to do? Quit school, go on welfare? Keep begging Zalman for money?"

"Whatever I want, there's a reason I can't get it. I just feel like I have no control over my life." Nikki smashed her cup into the wall. Ilana went white, then fled to the bedroom and shut the door.

And still nothing's changed, Nikki thought bitterly, remembering. Except now my summer's been taken away. Dammit, why did she tell her mother to come?

As the time approached, Nikki grew more agitated. "I know your mom just wants to break us up," she complained.

"Look, I haven't seen my mother in ten years. It's very important for me to work on my relationship with her."

"Ten years! You were there two summers ago, when we first got together! When she called to tell you your father had cancer and you should rush home right away. And of course you picked up the kids and ran to Jerusalem."

"Well, it might have been a cancer. They made a biopsy."

"He was just fine. And they spent the summer haranguing you, to go back to Zalman."

"It was pretty awful," Ilana admitted. "My mother and my grandmother both. They said they'd take Zalman anytime, he was a million times better than both their husbands. 'He makes a good living. He doesn't drink or gamble or go with other women. What more can you ask for?'"

"Love. Affection. Respect."

"That's why I want her to come here, *bulbul*. So she can see for herself. So we can talk, woman to woman, without my father's influence on her."

"So that's why he's not coming?"

"My father? He's not even speaking to me."

Nikki wondered why Mr. Katinsky even allowed his wife to come. She gathered that he made the rules at home. "My mother was a terrific cook," Ilana used to say. "She took the little allowance he gave her and made wonderful things, like a real delicatessen. When my father came home, he'd taste, and half the time he'd go 'Pfui!' and spit it out. And march off to a card game. Sometimes I think he just wanted an excuse to play cards. He's crazy for gambling."

"I guess your mom will have a better time without him," Nikki mused. "She'll probably want to see the sights — Fisherman's Wharf and the cable cars."

Ilana laughed. "She'll be happy just to go shopping. You don't know what it's like in Israel. If you find what you want it costs ten times as much, because of the import tax. But most of the time it's not even in the stores."

Mrs. Katinsky arrived on the appointed day, with two suitcases. She was fairer than her daughter, stout, yet with a pinched look about her face. Nikki wondered if she'd ever had Ilana's lushness, her wild energy, and if it was war or married life that crushed them out of her.

Their greetings were awkward. Nikki offered a compliment; Ilana translated. Mrs. K. seemed unimpressed. After a cup of tea, she said she was sleepy. Ilana put her in Tali's bed.

During the next few days, Nikki found they could communicate even when Ilana wasn't present. In addition to her native Yiddish and Polish, Mrs. K. had learned the languages of Poland's conquerors. Nikki remembered a few words from her childhood, folk songs and fragments of a Berlitz language course. So they groped for equivalents, a snippet of Hebrew or German or Russian, and what emerged was a phrase book collage.

But the kids spoke no Hebrew, not even Shimon, who'd eavesdropped on his parents' arguments for years and understood a lot more than he let on. Mrs. K. grieved over her inability to talk with them. Nikki felt a twinge of sympathy. Her own grandmother had never learned English, had grown old and died in New York cut off from her posterity.

"She wants me to bring them back to Israel," Ilana said, "so she can see them growing up. And I want them to go. Do you know how I feel when Shimon says he has to salute the flag in school? The American flag? Or worse, when he wants a Christmas tree?"

"I survived American schools, and we didn't have a Christmas tree. But it was just awful being a dyke in the '50s, and that's what Israel is like right now. How are *we* going to survive?"

"Well, we can't do it without help. Don't you understand, that's why we need her support."

Nikki thought she understood. There was a Hebrew word, *proteksia*. It meant you got jobs, apartments, black market goods through relatives or friends, and that way alone.

She couldn't believe they'd get proteksia from Mrs. K., but she decided to play the part of a good daughter-in-law. Every morning she squeezed fresh juice for everyone, cooked cereal or eggs and toast and went to work. When she came home Ilana had dinner ready, and Nikki played with the kids or took them out for ice cream afterwards. They seemed quieter than usual, withdrawn from her. If she asked them how the day had gone, the answer was always the same: "Grandma took us shopping."

Ilana also withdrew. When Nikki reached out to hug her, she froze, even when Mrs. K. was asleep. When Nikki complained, Ilana said, "Look, I can't give you anything right now. Right now my mother is my top priority. Just take care of your own needs. Pretend I'm not here." When Mrs. K. was up, they had passionate conversations in the livingroom. In Hebrew. In Polish. Incomprehensible. Once Nikki asked what they were talking about and Ilana said, "She wants me to buy a new sofa."

"What for?" Theirs was grimy and torn but it had great springs, a junk shop special they'd lugged home and covered with a bedspread.

"She says it's ugly," Ilana replied. "She's ashamed that I moved out from Zalman's big house into such poverty."

"What's the point of a new couch? The kids use it as a trampoline. Let them have fun — we'll get something nice when they're domesticated." It's a generational thing, Nikki thought, remembering her mother's livingroom set, the one from Macy's that took them two years to pay off. Her mother kept the plastic covers on for months.

There was more to those conversations than couches, but all Nikki got was a word here and there and one phrase, which Mrs. Katinsky repeated often and with great heat, something that sounded like "the cart o'tea belove."

Then Mrs. K. began to cook and clean the house. When Nikki got home from work dinner was on the table, and before she finished eating, Mrs. K. jumped up and started the dishes. The laundry was always done, her shirts were pressed and hanging in the closet. It was almost too easy. Nikki began to feel as though she were the guest. All she had to do was get up and leave for work.

The office was no refuge, though. Mr. Valdt had installed a program that counted every stroke on the word processor, and fired the sweet young manager for falling behind on her receivables. He'd hired a woman like himself, secretive and frosty. She and the other typist ignored Nikki's tentative "good morning"; they stared meaningfully at the clock when she went to the ladies' room.

During breaks she escaped into Jeff's office. "What's with those two?" she asked. She'd assumed the women would be her natural allies, yet they assiduously cut her dead, while

Jeff was her only real friend at the company.

"What do *you* think?" he said.

"I dunno. I guess they don't like how I dress." Nikki showed up in slacks, a Western blouse and walking shoes, while the other women wore cocktail dresses and four-inch heels. Each day different outfits, each worth a week's wages. Nikki couldn't imagine who they were trying to impress, since as far as she knew all the male employees were married. "But why are they ticked off at me? I'm not after their jobs or their boyfriends. I'm only here till Labor Day weekend, then I'm back in school."

"They know you're doing graduate work?" Jeff asked. She nodded.

"Well, they don't like that either. Those little bitches — excuse me Nikki, I know it's sexist — but they can't stand to see another woman move up out of the typing pool. The gal before you was going to college at night and they drove her out in less than three months. G.Y.A., honey. Guard Your Ass."

"Thanks." She went back to her typing, sure she could hang in till September. Or at least through Mrs. Katinsky's visit.

On Saturday morning she asked Ilana to go to the movies. "Since your mom is here, she can watch the kids. We haven't had a night out in weeks."

"You can't expect her to babysit," Ilana said. "She can't talk to the kids. If god forbid something happens, how can she call the police and say what's wrong?"

"Well, isn't it Zalman's turn to take them?"

"And her too? I can't leave her alone. She'll be terrified. Look, if you need time out, go to your studio."

So Nikki took Mrs. K. to the movies instead. They saw a Russian film with English subtitles, something very senti-mental, and Nikki cried at the end. They talked a little. As they were coming home, Mrs. K. said, "Please understand. I have nothing against you. You're a nice person. But you don't have money. And you're not a man."

On the way home Mrs. K. complained of bursitis in her shoulder. Nikki got out the Tiger Balm.

"*Ma zeh?*"

"It's Chinese medicine. Here, I'll rub it in for you."

Mrs. Katinsky blushed. She took the ointment and shut the bedroom door. Even the thought of me touching her freaks her out, Nikki told herself.

She lay awake that night, not even trying to put her arms around Ilana, who was sleeping soundly at the far edge of the bed. Thinking about Zalman the accountant, son of an accountant, a real prince, a great catch for a girl whose father ran a hardware store. Thinking about Mrs. K. so desperate for this marriage that she baked little treats for Zalman and passed them off as Ilana's. Thinking until a needle of pain began to throb in her left temple and over her eye.

The next day Mrs. K. went shopping with Ilana again. She bought a present for Nikki, a plaid Western shirt with mother-of-pearl snaps. The style was right but it was bright green and too tight around the chest. Nikki thanked her anyway. Then she went out with Shimon to shoot baskets in the playground.

"How do you like your grandma?" she asked, trying to be casual.

"She's okay," Shimon said. "She doesn't bug me. But she tries to tell Mom what to do."

"Yup." She shot off the board, missed, caught the ball and passed it. "You understand what they're saying?"

"A little. They talk too fast." He dribbled, spun around and jumped. Again the ball fell short.

"What's *the cart o' tea belove?*"

"Huh?"

"It's Hebrew. I think." She imitated Mrs. K. as best she

could.

"Oh," he said, "*ba-LEV. Dakart oti ba-lev*—it means, 'you stabbed me in the heart.' "

Nikki's stomach lurched sideways. She stood with the ball in her hands.

"What's the matter?"

"I'm not feeling so hot, kid. Is it okay if we stop playing now?"

On Monday the headache was worse and aspirin didn't help. There were codeine tablets in the bathroom cabinet, leftovers from a wisdom tooth extraction. Nikki took two and slipped the vial in her pocket. Then she locked the door, turned on the exhaust fan and smoked a joint, and by the time she got to work the pain was distant enough so she could function.

Mr. Valdt was out of town and the manager stared at her balefully when she rushed in at 8:03. The secretary didn't look at her at all. At ten o'clock she hid in Jeff's office but had to return to her desk when break was over.

By mid-afternoon Nikki was hiding behind the Xerox, feeding reports in one sheet at a time. It was a matter of enduring each moment, drop by drop, until five o'clock. She felt she was being squeezed into the smallest possible space and then pushed off the edge.

During the night the pain shifted to her right temple. It was there again the next day, and either the codeine wasn't working anymore or the pain was wearing her down.

"I've got a terrific headache," she said.

"There's aspirin in the cabinet," Ilana said abstractedly.

On Tuesday Nikki said she was feeling sick and left work early. No one was home when she got there and she rolled another joint. She was sitting in the kitchen, smoking and staring out the window when Ilana arrived with her mother.

"*Ma zeh po?*" Mrs. Katinsky asked.

Ilana looked distressed but she tried to answer casually. "It's just a little marijuana. Like taking a glass of wine."

Mrs. K. shook her head and said nothing.

Later that night, Nikki complained that she was having a hard time on the job.

"Look, I just can't listen to your problems," Ilana replied, her voice starting to break. "I haven't had a minute to myself for weeks. When I'm not with my mother I'm with the kids. Constantly. Twenty-four hours a day. I can't think, I can't even pee without somebody yelling a question through the door." For a moment Ilana looked like she was going to cry, but then she yanked her desk drawer open and took out a pack of cigarettes.

"I thought you stopped smoking," Nikki said.

Ignoring her, Ilana lit up. She took a deep breath and blew out a stream of smoke. "Right now," she said in a tight determined voice, "the most important thing is trying to work things out with my mother. And this is her last week in America."

The next day Mr. Valdt returned. He called Nikki into the office. She'd spent all afternoon xeroxing one report. She took long breaks. She'd taken advantage of his absence to slough off on the job, and didn't she realize that other people were keeping an eye on the shop while he was gone?

She said she understood it very well and because of those people she was resigning, effective immediately.

The apartment was very quiet. Most of the neighborhood kids were at summer school or the beach. Ilana and Mrs. K. were shopping, and Nikki had plenty of time to pack her clothes.

Her studio was in downtown Oakland, the penthouse of an old Victorian that had survived the first earthquake, been subdivided and decayed. The current manager slowed the decline by chasing the junkies out at gunpoint, but they'd already left their mark, setting fire to the bathroom while cooking up a fix. There was no shower. The only sink drained through a broken pipe into a slimy bucket and when it was full Nikki emptied it down the toilet. She rented the place for seventy-five dollars a month, and the manager turned a blind eye to her sleeping there illegally.

The gas line had been disconnected when a fire inspector came in to enforce the code, so she filled a kettle at the bathroom sink and turned on the hot plate. She had two more tabs of codeine with her tea, smoked another joint and threw herself in bed.

That evening she called Ilana. "I can't stand it anymore," she said. "I'm at the studio."

The reply was terse, angry. "Okay. Whatever you need."

The throbbing in her head went on for two more days. Occasionally she went downstairs to the corner chop suey house for soup or picked up yogurt at the deli. Mostly, she lay there watching the light come and go through the pink and yellow curtains, old sheets that she and Ilana had tie-dyed in a sunburst pattern, back when they first fell in love.

More than just a workshop, the studio had been their haven on those weekends when Zalman took the kids. Nikki put most of her decorating efforts into the bedroom, covering the blackened ceiling with a madras bedspread, the water stains on the walls with drawings, the floor with pillows and a threadbare oriental rug. She'd made an altar with feathers, shells and chunks of driftwood they'd found on the beach together. There, with the aid of music and candles, they forgot the fire scars and trash in the halls and entered a dreamtime of sensual delight.

It had been a long time since she felt that way. Nonetheless she curled up under the comforter and dozed on and off until the pain diminished to an occasional tic. She got up and browsed through the stack of unfinished paintings, rearranged her brushes and the precious little tubes of oil. How could she live on a part-time job in Israel, when everyone else worked six days a week and spent Shabbat in the clamor of family life?

The kids will wonder what happened to me, she thought. She went to the bathroom, splashed water on her face and combed her hair. I'll call Kelly Girls, she told herself. They pay less than Variola, but it's less hassle.

She went downstairs and drove to Ilana's apartment. Mrs. K. was packing to go to the airport. "Look," said Nikki clumsily, "I don't have anything against you. It's between me and Ilana."

"Yes," Mrs. K. said, nodding. "Well, goodbye." Then Ilana took her away.

When Ilana returned they made dinner and watched a cop show with the kids, tucked them in and told them stories till they fell asleep. Then Ilana went to the bedroom to work on her dissertation. After a while Nikki came in after her.

"Ilana," she began. "I did what you said. I needed to take my space."

Ilana looked up out of those coffee-colored eyes that were almost twins of her own. But the fiery liquid had congealed, had turned to black ice. Ilana had gone through a door and shut it between them.

"You abandoned me," she said. "I needed you, and you abandoned me."

Melina:
An Echo on the Line

SUE KATZ

MELINA CALLED from Cleveland, Ohio, and left a message on my machine here in Tel Aviv to call back. I didn't really want to call: she owed me letters so I didn't even know that she had moved from L.A. back with her folks, and anyway, I try to avoid the habit of calling international. But, in the hopes that she was off junk finally, maybe even off methadone, I called. And besides, although her message sounded upbeat, her health is always on my mind because she had been found HIV positive a few years back.

Melina is one of the hottest women I have ever loved. Our first meeting was like something out of a porn novel, except that it truly happened. I was in a mixed gay and bisexual bar in 1972, the kind of place I would never have taken my bulldagger self if I hadn't had a date with someone — we'll call her L — who insisted on us meeting there. Well, half-way into the evening, someone from L's collective rushed into the bar to say that their commune had just been busted and L took off to take care of business. I figured to finish up my ginger ale and get the hell out of there. The place was full of gays and straight swingers, the kind of California hips who slum in bi-bars in order to add some voyeuristic spice to their store of anecdotes and fantasies. I felt out of place in that loose scene.

As I lifted the glass to my lips, I saw this beauty on the far side of the room. She was the first woman I ever saw with a diamond in her nose, a very big nose, a very small diamond. She was wearing a halter top tied at the cleavage, her huge eyes were ringed with kohl, and she was looking up at me over the heads of the dancers. We held the proverbial glance across a crowded room, but then my superego imposed: That woman's no lesbian. She's just slumming it; get the fuck out of here. But before I could settle the glass back on the bar, she was at my shoulder.

"Buy you a drink?" she flirted.

"Don't drink," I said.

"What's in that glass, then?" she asked.

"Ginger ale."

She knew, like I knew, that if I really wasn't interested I wouldn't have answered. She ordered a beer for her and a ginger ale for me.

"I gotta go," I told her.

"Let's just have this one drink together, and then do what you want," she insisted.

"You're not Jewish," I said.

"No, Greek."

"You're not a lesbian," I said.

"But I'm not exactly straight," she answered. "Why don't we go to my place and I'll tell you about it."

"No way," I answered a bit too fast. "I was just leaving."

She had this way of looking up at me, even though there were no longer crowds between us, only around us, of making me feel tall, and I stood up even straighter. "How about a dance?" she offered.

"Sorry, I'm on my way out."

"Do you have a car?" she inquired. "Could you drop me off at home?"

"I'm probably not going your way." I knew this girl was trouble. She was as beautiful as Sophia Loren coming out of the water, as sexy as a professional, and I knew my collective would never permit it.

"Great," she complained, taking my measurement like a psychologist, "you're just gonna leave me to hitch home all by myself this late at night."

When we got to her place, she asked me in. I sat at the steering wheel as stiff as a new hardback. "No," I said. "I really can't."

"What's the problem?" she asked. "Are you afraid of me? Don't like me?"

It was getting more dramatic than I intended, but no more than I felt. "I gotta get back to my collective. I know you're not a lesbian and I just can't see the point."

"Oh, you're safe with me. I just wanted to offer you the most amazing Jamaican gold, you know, for the ride home and all." She knew all my weak points.

As we entered her apartment I felt taller and taller, and I'm only five-three. It wasn't anything I was doing; she was pumping me up somehow, maybe in the way she looked at me with those eyes — my god, those eyes — as she opened the four locks on her front door. She led me into her room, or more accurately, onto her bed, a huge affair that totally dominated the place. The bed was covered by a velvet quilt with a thick fur throw over it. There was nowhere else to sit.

She lit the "J." I stayed perched on the bottom edge of the bed, while she sprawled at my back, against the headboard, and under that poster of Theda Bara dressed only in leather and brass. Next to Melina, Theda was only a whisper of a woman. I had never been so turned on by the mere sight of someone in my life.

We were soon stoned, so stoned that I knew if I didn't get to a phone soon, I wouldn't get there at all. So I stumbled to the hall to call home. "Listen, I'm gonna get in late."

"How'd it go with L?" Amber asked me. "You at her commune?"

"Uh, no, L got called away, some trouble with the police at their place, I think. No, I met someone else."

"Who'dya meet? Is she OK?" she asked suspiciously.

"I don't know, I'm checking it out. But I don't wanna come back yet."

"So why do you sound like that?" Amber asked. "Better come home and we'll check her out tomorrow."

"No," and it was not characteristic to say no in these situations, "I'll come later. I wanna do this thing."

"I don't like the sound of this. Where are you? What's the number there?"

I gave her the number, but by then Melina was next to me, nuzzling me, and as soon as I put down the receiver, she took it back off, stuck a pencil in the dial so the phone wouldn't buzz while off the hook, and led me back to her room.

Melina had pulled back the covers; the sheets were red satin. This is a true story, accurate to the least detail. She put on some music, white music, stuff I didn't know, and left the room. When she came back she was wearing a satin night-gown with lacy parts around the tits. But that was irrelevant. She could've been wearing a K-Mart shopping bag for all I could see beyond her eyes and nose.

"Hey," I told her, "I'm only gonna stick around long enough to sober up. I don't mess with straight girls."

So she told me about her getting it on once with her best friend. Frankly, it was not an impressive story. The boyfriends were watching and all. When she said she was cold, and kinda slithered into the envelope she had made when she had pulled back the corner of the quilts, I saw the revolver she had under her pillow. She put it under the bed, explained about the crazy smack dealer ex-lover who was hassling her, and patted the place next to her.

"No, I'm not staying," I said, keeping up the myth.

"Who said anything about staying?" she replied.

I was getting dizzy from the "J"; I was really stoned. So I laid down, in all my clothes, on top of the covers, and she snuggled and rippled next to me through all their thickness. When she got my shirt off, her cool was shaken for the first time. "You've got tits!" she exclaimed.

I just about jumped off the bed. "What the fuck did you expect! A fucking hairy carpet on my chest and a set of balls below?"

Why would I do this to myself, I thought. Straight girls always expect you to be a man, really. This was not going to be good for my mental health. But by the next morning, I knew it was going to be great for my endocrinal system; I was nearly dehydrated from loss of liquids.

Although it may be a little late, I'm gonna make a long story short. My collective had a fit the next day, because I had broken security, not only by messing around with a junky hetero, but also by being incommunicado all night. But within weeks Melina was part of us, daily becoming more politicized, eventually joining the collective and becoming central to all our lives. Our love affair only lasted a few months, but later she was with another collective member for years. When I moved to Israel, she was the only one from the collective to keep it together with me, and I never visited the States without we should see each other.

So I called Melina back that night. And what was her big news? She was home with her parents for the first time in twenty years, getting clean off drugs — that is, everything except methadone. And she met a guy she used to know from high school, and they're getting married. I told her I was glad she was with someone she cared about, but I couldn't get too worked up about marriage. I asked about her health. She mentioned in passing that after three years the clinic discovered that they had given her mistaken information about her test — she was in fact HIV negative! In passing, she mentions this. I have been living daily with the threat of AIDS over her fucking head. She's known she's OK for a couple of months already. She already had a lawyer working on the case to sue the clinic. It's not right that she didn't tell me on account of being too busy getting her daily sperm injection.

At this point the conversation began to remind me of those intercontinental calls where there is a delayed echo — except that there wasn't any screw-up in the line, only in us. We were having two different conversations.

She said, sulky, "You know, you're the only one who supported me when I went on methadone, and the only one who didn't give me a hard time when I started living with Louie" — ["Yeah, your homo lover who hated your cunt," I thought bitterly to myself.] — "And you were the only one who didn't put me down for tricking. I thought I could count on you."

"Yeah, sure," I answered, "and you're the only one who kept it together with me over all these years and miles. I can't believe you didn't let me know that in fact your life isn't in danger."

"But now you're making a scene because I'm getting married," she whined.

"No, I'm making a scene 'cause you didn't remember that I'm out here worrying. I mean, when we were last together a year ago, we were talking about your coming over here to live so I could take care of you."

"Oh, so you're jealous?!" she replied triumphantly.

"I'm hurt, Melina, I'm hurt. I should've been among

the first to know."

"Oh you and your principles. They just don't make room for my happiness."

I saw it was hopeless. And I realized that I was paying good money in order to fulfill the expectations she obviously had that I was gonna reject her — probably like other friends had done — for inviting the national and religious authorities into her underpants. I did feel betrayed; not by her engagement — or at least not primarily — but by her turning up after all these silent months in another state, by her leaving me helpless out here in the desert of the Middle East thinking she might be dying.

"Look, I don't even know your parents' new address," I said.

"Oh, you wanna hang up now?"

"Yeah, something like that."

"OK," she said, "I'll write you and send you the address."

That was a couple of years ago. I have not, of course, ever heard from her again. I have this picture of Melina on my wall, here next to the typewriter. She is standing in the corner of a white-tiled bathroom, wearing Blues Brothers dark glasses and an amazing boned, black lace push-up bra. No matter what mess her life was in, I have always fantasized that we'd get it back together someday. I have been her most faithful fan, I have loved her fat and thin, poor or poorer. I have wanted her all these years, yes, I have, but mostly I have wanted her on her feet. I've been had and I'm gonna take down that graven image.

A Tendency
Toward Rebelliousness

MERRIL MUSHROOM

1965

"MERRELE, DOLLINK, come in, come in." Tante Chana closed the door behind me, as I slipped into her Bronx apartment, grateful to get away from the cabbage smell of the hallway. I bent and hugged her small, stocky body. She took my face between her hands and gave me such a wet kiss on the mouth that I felt like I was smooching a half a grapefruit. Then, in the most loving gesture of all, she squeezed my cheek between her thumb and forefinger which, even though she was 83 years old and had arthritis, was a hard enough tweak to bring tears of pain springing forth. *"Oi, shi' madele!"* Her blue eyes shone with pleasure at my visit, and I grinned at her as hard as the ache in my cheek would allow. She pulled me toward the kitchen where her sister Rachel was cutting garlic into p'cha.

"So, how's our rebellious grandniece?" boomed Tante Rachel, as she pushed herself away from the kitchen table. Still holding the garlic knife, she stretched up onto her eighty-six-year-old toes, pulled my head down, and planted another of those tantele kisses halfway onto my lips.

"Fine, Tantele." I was so relieved that she didn't pinch my sore cheek too, I hardly minded that the kissed side of my mouth was beginning to feel as though a slug had crawled over it. This was the way my tantes' kisses had been for as far back as I could remember, and I always had let them dry on my face. My only alternative would have been to wipe them off, and no matter how young I was, I adored my tantes and never would have dreamed of hurting their feelings by wiping off their kisses, no matter how wet they were. "How are my rebellious great aunts?"

Chana snorted. "Listen to you!" She chuckled. "How about some p'cha?" Without waiting for an answer, she ladled a generous amount into a bowl and handed it to me with a spoon.

"Thanks." I dipped out a taste, then another. It was perfect — the calves' feet cooked until all the gelatin had dissolved, the bones scraped clean. Now Tante Rachel would add chopped vegetables and hard-boiled eggs, then leave the p'cha to set like jello so that we could slice it and eat it cold with rye bread and horseradish mustard. But I preferred p'cha before it was finished, when it was hot, the consistency of gumbo, and savory with garlic. I shared this liking for hot p'cha with my great aunts, as we also shared our tendency toward rebelliousness, especially against the standards of sex-appropriate behavior set by our parents, our religious culture, and society in general.

The tantes sat and watched me while I ate p'cha. Then, each of us fortified with a glesele tea, we retired to the living room to chat. Tante Chana sank into the armchair, Rachel seated herself on the straight chair, and I pulled over the rocker. "*Nu?* Any nice *maydeles* in your life these days?" asked Tante Chana.

My tantes knew about my dyke habits, although we did not discuss the subject in so many words. If I was considering getting serious about a woman I was dating, I'd bring her to meet my tantes, then ask them for their opinion of her. I think they approved, as neither of them had much use for men, and, more than that, they both really liked women. They still kept in touch with my ex-lover Ruby, calling her their other niece. Had they been born at a different time or into different circumstances, they might each have made a life with a woman lover. As it happened, they did not, but in a time when the man was unquestioned head of the household, neither of my tantes would be so controlled.

When Rachel and Chana were young girls in Lodz, Poland, just before the turn of the century, they refused to accept the rule of their father, a Hassidic Rabbi. Later, they would not obey their husbands, and finally, they refused even to obey the Russian Czar Nicholas himself. Because of their activity in the revolutionary movement, they were forced to flee Poland for their lives. This was fortunate in the long run, because they eventually escaped to the United States and were not lost to the Holocaust as were the family members they left behind.

Chana was the first of the sisters to defy her father. She had always been outspoken and quick-tempered. When she was fifteen years old, her father went to Ger with his brother-in-law Davidal. There, as was the custom, he formally betrothed Chana, without her knowledge, to the son of one of the prominent Gerer Hassidim. This was the way that marriages were made, had been made for generations, without question. After the bargain had been sealed before a *minyon*, Chana's father continued on to Brezen to meet his future son-in-law; while Davidal went straight back to Lodz to be the first to bring the good news to the family.

Chana, her mother, and her sisters were just finishing their meal when Davidal arrived. He danced over to the dish closet, snatched up a plate, dashed it to the floor, and broke it as was the custom on all festive occasions — to remind Jews

111

in the midst of our joy that the Holy Temple was destroyed. *"Mazel Tov!"* cried Davidal. "Chana is betrothed to a fine boy, one of the finest, the son of a great Hassid!"

Chana stood up, her eyes snapping. Three years earlier she had watched her sister Rachel married off to a man her father chose, and he turned out to be a *schlemiel* for whom nothing ever went right. She turned to her mother. "Make Uncle Davidal pay you for the plate he broke," she demanded. "I am not betrothed!" She glared at the surprised Davidal. "I will not let anyone choose a mate for me. If and when the time comes, I will do my own choosing!"

Davidal stared at her. He couldn't comprehend how a girl could talk to her own mother with such a mouth. Marriages among Hassidim were always arranged, either by a marriage broker or else directly between the fathers of the bride and groom. The women were not consulted. A girl was usually married by the time she was fourteen years of age, and she was not supposed to see her husband until they met beneath the wedding canopy. What did Chana mean, she wasn't betrothed? The engagement had been made before a full quorum of ten men, and a Jew's word before a quorum was binding. But he couldn't argue in front of his sister, so he went home.

When Chana's father returned home and heard of her decision to defy him, he had no choice but to take her before the Rabbi, who would act as a judge, since this was a matter that involved Jewish law in that the bargain had been made before a quorum. The Rabbi asked Chana, "Maiden, is it your wish to break this engagement?"

"Yes," Chana replied, "it is."

The Rabbi turned to Chana's father. "The Talmud says that a person has no right and so is forbidden to marry off a child against the child's will. Therefore, I release you from your promise before the quorum and declare this engagement void." Chana had won!

Tante Rachel had been married at age fifteen to a baker whom her father had chosen for her. I had heard the family gossip that she had divorced him, an almost unspeakable act, but I never knew the whole story. I decided that now was the time to ask. First I answered Tante Chana, "No new *maydeles, tante,*" then turned to Tante Rachel. "Tante, one thing I always wanted to know . . ."

"*Vas?*"

"Did you come over with the baker?"

"No, dollink. I divorced that s*hmigege,* that fool, back in Poland."

"Tell, Tante . . ." I begged, wanting to hear about it.

Tante Rachel took a long drink of her tea. "Vell, it happened in 1903. I lived then in a two-room flat in Lodz with mine husband the baker and our four children, your mother's cousins. We were in the midst of a revolution against the Czar Nicholai. One day mine sister Esther came to me. I must help her, she said. She was always rebellious, too, mine sister Esther was. Now she was making speeches for the revolution that were bringing young people into the movement in droves; so now the police were looking for her. She was no longer safe living at home with Mother and Father, and she wanted to know if she could move in with me. It was not that I, her sister, would be so much safer, but my flat was a good place to be — easy to post lookouts and with good escape routes out the back. Of course I told her yes, and shortly after Esther came, my sister Dora moved in, too. So good a safe place that flat was, that the workers started to have their meetings there. The flat became so crowded sometimes that I had to send the children to stay with Mother.

"Mine husband the baker did not approve one bit, let me tell you. One day he yelled at me, 'Rachel, we must put a stop to this nonsense! I will talk to mine father-in-law! I will make a *shandeh,* a scandal! I will even report to the police if it does not stop!'

"I would listen to no more out of the mouth of that fool. Something inside me was changing, and I had many new ideas in my head. I shook mine finger at the baker. 'You will report to the police, will you? You will become an informer? Do you know what they do to an informer? They find him, and then they cut out his tongue!'

"Mine foolish husband lost all his courage now. He became terrified for the safety of his tongue. His face turned pale, and he whined, 'So who said I was going to become an informer?' and he ran out of the house and back to his bakery.

"But I was too angry to stop. I followed him. 'If you don't like what I am doing, you can divorce me,' I yelled at him.

" 'So who wants to divorce you?'

"Now I was even angrier. 'You *will* divorce me. I've had enough of you and your foolish talk. My father married me off to a piece of *dreck,* and I've had enough of it!'

"Then he started to plead, 'David's daughter, don't be angry with me. Maybe I'm not the smartest man in the world, but I am your husband, and I want you.'

"This irritated me even more. 'Your wanting me is not enough,' I told him. 'I have to want you, too, and I do not want you.' And from that day on, I did not allow him to come near me again.

"So, two weeks later, mine husband dusted the flour off his round hat, shook the flour off his long coat, and went to see mine father. 'Did you ever hear of a Jewish woman chasing her husband away from her bed?' he asked.

" 'Maybe she is unwell,' Father answered.

" 'No, she is not unwell, she just does not want to live with me. She told me so herself.'

" 'And what do you want me to do?'

"'You are her father. Talk to her. You gave her to me, now make her live with me.'

"'That would be against the wise laws of our Talmud,' said Father. 'If she does not want you, I am not allowed under Jewish law to force her to live with you.'

"So then we went to the Rabbi, and he granted us a divorce, and I was well rid of that fool."

I laughed appreciatively, loving the fact that I came from a line of hot, spunky, Jewish women. *"Nu,"* said Tante Chana, "how about some lunch, dollink? I have a fresh rye bread and a nice whitefish . . . but speaking of fish reminds me . . ." She hesitated, and I grinned with glee at the propect of another tante meiseh before we ate.

The Woman
Who Lied

JANO

SHE MEANT to tell the truth, but she lied. She didn't mean to. The lie was so minute, so unintentional, like some awkward crumb that grazes your cheek. But this was only the beginning.

It goes like this.

Hannah and Yetta are lovers. And it is new, like the smell of warm bread. They stumble and poke over each other's bodies looking for sweet spots. Yetta thinks she finds two — Hannah's nipples. Yetta squeezes Hannah's long soft nipples and whispers, "Nu? Yes?"

But Hannah feels nothing — nothing but the desire to please Yetta. So she mumbles, "Nu, yes."

Instantly her nipples grow hard and erect. Hannah eyes her nipples and laughs. This is very amusing to Hannah because she feels nothing. Yetta, on the other hand, mistakes Hannah's laugh as a sign of pleasure and begins kneading even more. Now Hannah's nipples are pulsating. They rise wildly. It's as if some she-dybbuk has crawled under Hannah's ear, points to her nipples, and scolds, "This will teach you, Hannah Levin, to rise above the truth."

Then the dybbuk giggles and moans some mysterious chant in Yiddish, which of course echoes out of Hannah's mouth. Yetta gasps joyfully and chants back. She wraps Hannah's nipples around her fingers and rocks and sucks.

Hannah's nipples rise again. They forsake their nipple shapes and ooze from her breast like coils of pastry dough. They swirl and float overhead. They circle Hannah's body and playfully touch themselves. Quickly, they swoop down, and alight atop Hannah's breasts — now two perfect, warm crusty bagels.

Hannah is bewildered, but silent. Yetta does not see Hannah, only her delicious nipple-bagels.

"If only I had cream cheese," she murmurs while she chomps the firm crust.

Now the nipples leap up. They undo their circular shapes and dance and stretch and bulge into curvaceous, bulbous forms.

"Vey is mir!" Hannah exclaims, "my nipples they are braids of challah!"

"Not mere braids of challah, Hannahala," the dybbuk sneers, "challah bobbe meisehs, Hannahala."

Then the dybbuk blows the sweet smell of challah straight into Yetta's nostrils. Yetta is *fershimmeled* by the challah smell. She squeals and wildly swings the nipple-braids overhead, like lassos.

Hannah calms Yetta down, "Shah, Yetta, the Sabbath is coming."

"Hannah, I will make good use of your challah for the Sabbath."

She delicately weaves nipple-garlands for Hannah's hair. Then with more nipple, she fashions an ornate breastplate for her chest. Next comes tefillim straps for Hannah's arm in case she should want to *daven*.

Hannah pleads, "Yetta, quickly, the Sabbath is coming, let's make Shabbos."

"We can use more of your challah for the *motzi*," Yetta announces.

Hannah nods reluctantly and drags her nipples to the table. They light the Shabbos candles. As Hannah's hands beckon the light of Shabbos into her eyes, she instantly knows she can no longer *shlep* such a burden around.

"Yetta, we must break this bread," Hannah says gravely. "These nipples are not really mine. They are *bobbe meisehs*. You do bring me pleasure but not in those places."

They hug and chant the *motzi*: *"Hamotzi lechem min ha' aretz."* Who bringest forth bread from the earth.

They tear soft hunks of challah off of Hannah. Instantly the braids become brittle and stale and both challah-nipples snap from her breast. Her own soft nipples reappear.

Hannah is relieved. *"Zi g'zunt."*

Yetta is sad and hurt, but she whispers, "After dinner, Hannah, we'll just have to find those other places."

Soup Story

ELLEN GRUBER GARVEY

NAN STIRRED THE SOUP, waiting for Michelle to be late. She had already made plans against annoyance: Certainly a trip between two such different parts of Michelle's life couldn't be an easy one; naturally Michelle would have trouble getting away from her family's lengthy farewells in time to leave for her lover's house.

On the subway, where Nan's imagination didn't follow her, Michelle had hesitated, indecisive: Should she continue on toward Nan's or go alone through the rain to her own apartment?

Nan wiped the window fog with the edge of her flowered apron and watched Michelle's ponchoed figure grow larger coming up the street. Finally full-sized, Michelle dropped onto Nan's kitchen couch, a drowning victim rescued from icy rain and family undertow. A small river ran down the middle of the kitchen from her wet shoes. Across it, Nan was stirring soup. Michelle watched her distant figure from the opposite bank and shivered, chilled and hungry in the warm kitchen.

"Hungry? Really? After visiting your mother? That seems bizarre somehow, against nature." Nan's voice seemed loud, too close.

"If she'd been too busy with her own life to bother cooking it would have been fine. I'd have been glad to bring my own peanut butter sandwich."

"Ha." Nan wiped her hands on her apron, dipped a spoon into the pot. "It's just as well you're hungry. There seems to be all this food for some reason." Nan's gesture included the pot, evidently made fuller by Michelle's lateness, the necessity of feeding soup to Michelle heightened.

The drowning victim watched Nan put the cover on the soup pot, far away. Was there some safe way across the distance to Nan? She shook herself free of the couch, moved her shoes to the radiator and crossed the stream that remained. "What is it you're making?" Michelle hugged Nan from behind, resting her chin on Nan's shoulder to see what the world looked like from there. It was full of cooking pots. Michelle pointed to an idle one. "This pot here, that appears to contain nothing. What's in here?"

"It's for the matzah balls. Here, put water in it."

The rebellion of the pipes filled the kitchen. "Ah yes," said Michelle. "Matzah balls. I've seen the vast fields where they ripen slowly. Amber waves of matzah balls."

"The great steppes of California," said Nan.

"I bet I know how you make it. You cook the matzah balls until the water becomes a rich broth, discard those matzah balls that have lost their flavor, add a dash of this seltzer, and eat the wonderful tasty soup. An old family recipe? Here."

Nan took the pot from her. "*That* explains why my Aunt Deena's tasted so awful. But if you look closely you'll see there's a chicken involved here. The seltzer actually *is* for the matzah balls — you put it in, my mother says it makes them lighter. Matzah balls of the light matzah ball school of thought."

"My mother makes them heavy, with a surprise inside."

"Something substantial? A check?"

"Nuts and raisins, I think. She hasn't made it for a long time. I don't remember." Michelle sank back on the couch across the kitchen and pulled an old blanket from behind the cushions. "When I think of it there's a lot she hasn't cooked in a long time. It's part of what's so upsetting. Like today, for lunch, she crams me into the kitchen and there's this plate of burnt pot roast and little bits of leftovers getting moldy. She always does it with food." Michelle wrapped herself into a tight bundle inside the blanket.

"Could you move over? I have to get in there." Bits of dried herbs floated down onto Michelle from the cabinet above her as Nan rummaged. Nan stepped down from the couch, apron billowing, bearing pepper. "Does what with food?"

"Uses it like that. When I dropped out of college the first time and they were so unhappy about it, they told me okay, it's your life, your problem. Then the next time I came home they were keeping a canary in my old room and all they had in the house to eat was nuts and seeds. They were on a special diet, my mother said. They kept calling me in to hear the damned bird whistle." The faucet, half off, half on, whined resentfully again. Nan turned the water on full force. Michelle continued: "After that I gave up playing the flute, you know, for five years. So now it's like a message; when they start stinting on the food it's clear they disapprove of something I'm doing." Michelle shrugged, lay back. The kitchen smelled like her own family's: soup, onions, chicken; the smell of aunts and cousins poking, prying, commenting on her flute playing until the cooking smells choked her and she couldn't breathe enough to play. "In your kitchen — it's such a familiar smell. Like relatives." Michelle pulled the blanket into a cocoon around her, shut her eyes.

"Oh yes, it's like my aunt's." Nan inhaled, alerted to pleasing memories of listening unnoticed to her own aunts, busy among themselves with their stories. She smiled and looked over at Michelle. The steamed lenses of Michelle's glasses hid her eyes, but the rest of her face seemed pinched, the lips held tight at the corners — the kind of expression that would stick to a face and then get wrinkles to prop it up. She put her hand to Michelle's cheek to smooth it. Michelle started; her eyes opened to the expanse of Nan's flowered apron over her, and Nan's face, more concerned than the worst aunt. Michelle's mouth pinched tighter.

"How can you see anything with your glasses like that?" Nan retreated to the other end of the couch, still concerned.

"Glasses? They were perfectly clean when I came in here. If you wipe them too often they get scratched."

"No wonder you're in a bad mood with everything so dusty in front of you. This stuff won't scratch." Nan pulled her shirt tail from under her apron and leaned toward Michelle, her hand full of plaid flannel.

"Would you stop it?"

"All right, all right." Nan polished her own glasses. "See? A much more attractive world this way."

Silence from the other end of the couch. Michelle crossed her arms to stare at the peaceful expanse of blank wall, away from Nan.

"Sorry," said Nan. "Okay?" At the stove, shirt tucked behind her apron, Nan got down the chopping board, set it as far away from Michelle as possible. "Your folks. About them disapproving. What do you think it is this time?"

Michelle let out the breath she'd been holding and looked up to see Nan's face on the other side of the kitchen, no longer unbearably concerned, but just interested. She relaxed against the couch arm. "It's pretty obvious, don't you think?"

Michelle untangled one hand from the blanket and waved it, as though conducting, while she spoke. "When I got there it was 'Oh your cousin Cheryl's coming after lunch with her fiance. This is the third one, now, it looks serious. I got so busy cleaning the house I didn't want to get it dirty again cooking. No, don't bring the pot roast in there, we'll eat in the kitchen, at the counter.' I felt like some poor relation being handed food out the back door — you know, 'eat the soup over the sink, it might spill.'"

"That's terrible. Didn't you say anything?" Nan laid the scallions out in straight lines on the board. She cut them carefully and scientifically, making small cross sections.

"My mother kept walking around with the vacuum. 'He's a doctor,' she says. 'Cheryl's very involved. We want everything nice for when they come.' The fact that I had dragged myself all the way from Brooklyn didn't count; that was expected. The point was for Cheryl to catch a husband. Then when the two of them showed up, they treated him like a king." Michelle shook her head.

"You should have brought me along. I would have told your mother not to be mean to you." Nan emptied the board full of scallions into the dark green bowl on the counter. Pale green and white against dark green: A summer meadow, there, in the middle of her kitchen.

"God knows how they would have acted if you came." Michelle's voice was cold. Nan looked up from her meadow.

"Well it's not as if she doesn't know about me by now, or at any rate about you. How could she miss it?"

"No," Michelle pressed the rough blanket fringe against her chin to think. "The point with them seems to be that I'm not fulfilling their expectations in a negative sense — *not* having a boyfriend, *not* being married. I don't think they get any further than that. They just don't ask about relationships and I don't tell them."

"What about when somebody they know asks them? What do they tell the relatives?"

"Oh, they present it as 'Well Michelle's so busy with her flute she doesn't have time for that sort of thing.'" She pulled the blanket closer around her. "I guess they really think that. It seems like an okay way to deal with a potentially tense and difficult situation."

The chopping board balanced evenly in Nan's hands, its weight distinct. "And then you all politely acknowledge the potential tension and difficulty? You congratulate yourselves on your maturity in handling it so well?"

"Well what's wrong with that? We don't want to talk about it so we don't talk about it." Michelle's back was pressed against the back of the couch, her legs drawn up protectively. "Why does that give you the right to attack me?"

Nan turned away, stared at the counter. A roach was running across the back of it. She raised the chopping board and slammed it down. The roach scurried away; the green bowl crashed from the edge of the counter to the floor, scattering china shards and scallions.

"Shit." Nan grabbed for the refrigerator as she slid on the scallions.

"Oh dear," said Michelle. She drew her legs further up, away from the sharp fragments on the floor as Nan planted her feet on secure ground and let go of the refrigerator.

"You know what the matter is?" said Nan. "You go to your parents' house and all you can think about is being the daughter they want." Plaid flannel sleeves unrolled themselves as Nan gestured; she rolled them back up. "Then when you're done pretending over there you come back here and you want it to be all the same. Well it's not. You wanted to ignore me while you were over there and now you still want to ignore me."

"I'm not ignoring you. We've been talking. I haven't

been sitting here reading the paper. Anyhow, how do you know what I did at my parents'?"

"See? You've just been telling me what you did. You don't care what we talk about. You don't care what I think. You don't really see me anyway."

"Oh for god's sake." Michelle took off her glasses, wiped them on her shirt. "There, is that better?"

"They're your glasses." Nan sat on the other end of the couch, arms around her knees. The chunk of bowl at her feet was from the edge, where a spoon could rest while aunts bustled companionably with pots in their hands. "I liked that bowl." Nan's voice was muffled in her apron. "It was my grandmother's. We used to eat matzah ball soup out of them in the kitchen there. Now I just have one left."

"I'm sorry." Michelle worked her bare feet into her damp shoes. "I'll help sweep up. Though how you can lust after your family's kitchens is beyond me."

Nan kept her head down.

"Look. I don't think I've been ignoring you, even with my parents. But why should I go out of my way to make friction while I'm there? They can think what they want. It makes them happy, so why not?"

"But they already know. Your mother isn't exactly polite to me when I answer the phone at your house at seven in the morning. If you cared, you'd make things clear to them."

"You mean if I loved you enough I'd make them accept you? Come on."

"If you cared enough about yourself you'd want them to accept *you*. It has nothing to do with me." Nan's hands floated up, palms outward, disclaiming responsibility.

Michelle stopped tying her shoes, pulled the blanket back around her. "What is this, a campaign? We should all be one happy family? I thought being a lesbian meant I wouldn't have to put up with all that. I don't want them in my life. It's not about you. It has nothing to do with you."

"So why is what they want so important to you?"

"It's not that. I've told you what they're like. If I tell them — my mother really — she'd just take it over somehow."

"What, she's going to start introducing you to woman doctors, nice woman lawyers?"

"It's just that she makes everything seem so depressing." Michelle glanced around Nan's kitchen; her eyes stopped at the refrigerator. "Like when she *does* serve dinner. In the refrigerator there all the food ends up tasting the same in ways it's not supposed to. Everything blurs into everything else."

Nan followed Michelle's gaze. The refrigerator of her own prying Aunt Deena hovered in view, everything jammed together. "Oh, I know what you mean." On the top shelf, the onions and garlic pressed their smells on the farmer cheese; below, all the foods shoved their opinions on the butter. Nan's voice lost its self-assurance. "You're right. It *is* unbearable."

"I just don't want to be that exposed to her. It would only make it worse."

"I'll get you a big roll of plastic wrapping stuff for your birthday. Look, it still might not make it worse. It might be very different from what you think."

"Miracles happen."

"I realize it's your decision. They're your parents. I know I was glad when I told my parents —"

"Yeah, but what about last week?" Michelle stood, got out the dustpan. "You didn't act so superior when your mother was starting in again on 'why aren't you through with this phase already?'"

"Well there's no insurance they won't backslide sometimes. But still, it changes what I can say — it elevates the level of discourse." Nan raised her feet and tucked up her apron as Michelle swept around the couch. "And no matter what, it was worth it for the dream I had afterward that there were no closets in my apartment and all my clothes hung from a ship's steering wheel instead. Actually," Nan closed one eye and appraised the room with the other, "it wasn't exactly like this apartment — it was sort of like yours too."

The scraping of the broom stopped; Michelle's breath came out in a hiss. "How inspiring. So now you're moving your *dreams* into my apartment too?"

"Hey. That was my dream and it *was* inspiring. Look, it's your business what you do about it. But you don't know how your mother would react. Maybe she'd make you a feast — she likes to cook, you said."

"Keep your fantasies to yourself." The broom raked the floor with quick, hard strokes.

"Why not? What annoys her about your being a lesbian is that she doesn't get to make you a wedding. Maybe she'd like to cook a nice dinner instead."

"I can just see her doing that." The smile that crossed Michelle's face left it softer. She rested a hand on Nan's knee and they sat side by side in silence. "You've got some other mother in mind there lady. But that's okay with me."

"No, it could happen." Nan stretched her legs out, settled her feet across Michelle's lap. "My Aunt Reizel once told me a story about that. She used to keep a small store in Chelm where she sold chickens. You know about Chelm, right?"

"Sure," said Michelle. "Most of my family must have come from there. Unless there was some other town of fools closer to Lithuania." Michelle's hand turned into a beak, fingers nipping Nan's pant leg. "So your aunt sold chickens, huh?"

Nan lifted the nipping hand, held it. "She sold other things too. But when there was an occasion, people would buy a lot of chickens. There were none of these catered affairs then, people had to cook for their own affairs — and for their serious

127

relationships as well. And marriages — well that was really something.

"So one time," Nan continued, "a customer comes into my Aunt Reizel's shop. This customer, Hodl, came to order provisions for the betrothal of her daughter Fruma Feigel to Hanneh the cook. In Chelm, this was a big occasion. Just because they didn't have catering doesn't mean it was some stick-in-the-mud town with no advanced ideas, you know.

" 'So,' says Hodl. 'What do you have for my daughter Fruma Feigel and for her Hanneh, she's like a daughter to me? Nothing but the best. I want only the plumpest chickens.'

" 'For you,' says Reizel, 'and for your lovely daughter and daughter-in-law, may they live long and happily, whether it be monogamously or in an open relationship, as they so choose, I have only the best. Feel these chickens —"

"I have a question," Michelle raised her free hand. "Did you Aunt Reizel really tell you all this? I can't quite see it."

"Always so suspicious. Of course she did. She was a remarkable woman, a wonderful storyteller. It's just that there were a few parts she didn't remember, so I have to add them.

"So Reizel holds up a chicken. 'Blow on the feathers,' she tells Hodl. 'See how yellow with fat in the back. These chickens will make a soup as rich as chicken fat itself.'

"Now Hodl was a suspicious type, always doubting. She gets all excited. 'But I want only the best for my two. For the joining of my dear Fruma Feigel to her dear Hanneh there should be nothing but her parents' glowing pride. Do you think I wouldn't spend the money for my daughter to have real chicken fat instead of something almost as good? Take away these chickens. I'll have nothing but the finest chicken fat.'

"So Reizel says, 'Of course, for your guests at this proud time you must serve the best, that they should toast the children's happiness with proper fervor. Naturally I have chicken fat — and the best, richest chicken fat you'll find anywhere. It's as golden as the pleasure your daughter is bringing you, as golden as pure olive oil.'

"'Again,' says Hodl. Hodl was very dramatic. 'Again you want to make me ashamed before the entire community. This is my pearl of a daughter who's being married and you offer me these dregs. How can you sell me chicken fat almost as good as olive oil? Bring me the olive oil itself.'"

"Somehow," said Michelle, "I get the feeling Hodl's a little ambivalent about her daughter marrying a woman."

"Aunt Reizel thought so too," said Nan, "but of course she had to sell the customer what she asked for. 'Hodl,' she says. 'Naturally you want to give your daughter and her intended the best, no matter what your opinion of Hanneh is. If olive oil is what you want, I'm the one to buy it from. This olive oil is as clear and free of ambiguities as your intentions. This olive oil is as pure as well water.'

"Reizel told me she wondered, maybe she phrased it too politely. But after all, she was a storekeeper, not a family counselor. And Hodl wasn't the type to take a hint and examine her motivations. So Hodl gets huffy. 'My pride in my little Fruma Feigel and my affection for her little Hanneh are only the clearest and purest. Why would I want anything but the best for them? You tell me this olive oil is almost as good as well water. How could I serve this knowing I could serve water? Bring me a barrel of the finest well water.'

"Reizel could see she had made up her mind, so what could she do? She called for the water carrier and Hodl walked proudly home with him rolling a barrel behind her." Nan's hands spread palms upward as she shrugged.

Michelle's smile had the graciousness of victory in it. "That's not much of a wedding feast Hodl ended up giving her daughter." She stood up, cheerful, shaking out blanket fringes.

"Nope. Not much nourishment. While you're up,

there are more scallions in the refrigerator. Your turn to chop."

Michelle rummaged through the vegetable bin. "Some celebration." She shut the drawer. "It has the ring of the inevitable to it. You really can't seem to get away from it." The rubber band holding the scallions together sprang away across the floor and disappeared.

"Well she may have meant well, even if she couldn't go through with it. Hodl had certain good qualities too, you know. But that's not really the way it ends." Watching Michelle's victorious smile fade, Nan crossed her arms under her apron top, resting her hands under the flowers. "When Hodl got home, she said to Fruma Feigel, 'Look how hard I work for you. I spent all day bargaining at the store so you should see how your parents lay themselves out for your happiness.' And Fruma Feigel was all ready to be grateful; she was so pleased that her mother was accepting her, her being with Hanneh. And so, although she always hated to hear about her mother's shopping trips, she made her sit down on the couch and take off her shoes; she brought her a cold glass of borscht and said 'Tell me all about it.'

"So Hodl said, 'Remember how at your cousin's wedding we had that lovely chicken soup, rich and golden and so clear? Well for you, nothing has been spared. I've worn my throat out shopping, and I've brought back the finest there is — a barrel of water.' "

"See."

"Quiet. When Fruma Feigel understood that her mother planned to drink to her happiness in water, she didn't say a word but went to Hanneh's house. And that night they packed, and the next day they moved to Brooklyn." Nan sat up on the couch, beaming.

"Good for them." Michelle's back pressed against the wall, her arms wrapped around her ribs. Scallion slices were huddled together on the chopping board in a ragged immigrant heap. "Why don't you invite them to dinner sometime."

"We could invite them right now. Just put those scallions in. It's all done."

Michelle raised the board to the pot, knife poised to scrape, and stopped. "Why did you have to marry them off like that?"

"What do you mean? They wanted to get married."

"I don't think they did. They seemed pretty ambivalent to me."

"That was the mother who was ambivalent. You don't really get to see them in the story."

"That's not what I remember. It was pretty clear to me that Hanneh and Feigel were both ambivalent." The knife returned to the stove top unused; the scallion-covered board descended from its position above the soup pot. "I don't think they really wanted to be married."

"I don't know where you get that. It was my story and that's not what I put in it. Anyway, even if they were ambivalent, that would mean they wanted to get married too, besides wanting not to. They would want both things."

"Well I just don't think they wanted to get married. I don't believe it." Michelle set the board and its scallions back on the counter.

"So that's not ambivalence, then. That's decision. But really, that's not what's in the story. Why are you opening the window? It's cold out."

"No, it's really not bad out at all."

The street below was quiet, empty.

Nan stood by the stove, watching Michelle's reflection in the window, night in back of it. "You look as though you expect to see someone out there."

Michelle picked up her now-dry socks from the radiator, moving quickly, speaking slowly. "No," she said. "No one out there. It's something — I remembered now, I just remembered. I forgot something at my house."

"Well what is it? Couldn't I lend you something?"

"No — I left something. I have to go home."

Nan lifted the last remaining green bowl. "Don't you even want some soup?"

"No. No soup."

The
Thirteenth Passenger

JUDITH STEIN

IT WAS A FLUKE, someone else in her seat, a moment's panic about the full plane, and then a seat in first class. Mollie's first feeling was one of relief — not just over having a seat, but over getting to sit for once in a seat that was actually wide enough. For a second she thought, "It must be OK to be fat in first class." Then she remembered that most people never thought it was OK to be fat. First class people just had more room to move than other people.

Mollie stretched in the seat. "What a pleasure!" she thought. Her luck continued: no one sat in the seat next to her. One wide orange plush seat and a whole aisle between Mollie and her nearest neighbors, the goyishe-looking honeymooners across the aisle. Huge plush seat-backs made a welcome barrier between herself and the two men directly in front of her. To top it all off, she was in the last row in first class, so she could avoid talking with the people around her. No forced sociability, just comfort and semi-solitude. Mollie was thrilled with her good luck.

For a while she wondered about the people in front of

her. At first she thought they were a couple; the smaller one a woman, smooth arm and small hand reaching up to play with the light, the air nozzle. Then this woman became the young man he really was, snuggling up to the much older man in the next seat. "Homosexuals!" Mollie thought with delight, forgetting for a moment all her reservations about man-boy love. She wondered how they could be so brazen, and decided it was because they were so rich. Then Mollie's fantasies were shattered as the plump woman in baby blue across the aisle got a blanket for herself, and one for the young man in front of Mollie. Quickly she realized it was a nuclear family: mom, dad and the kids, first class style. Mollie felt disappointed, then laughed at herself for inventing other gay people when none were there.

Shortly after take-off, the flight attendants began serving drinks. Mollie wondered if first class had male attendants all the time; if it was considered classier. When the drinks came, another surprise — no worn dollar bills changed hands. And the drinks were served in real glasses, not plastic cups. For a minute Mollie was sorry that she didn't drink, and had only asked for soda. After all, free liquor doesn't come too often. But she was glad to get the peanuts. "Eagle Brand Honey Roast Peanuts," she read on the fancy golden foil pouch. She was starving, but there were only eight nuts in the puffy bag dressed up fancy for first class flight. And they tasted just like ordinary beer nuts, good, but nothing special. Fortunately, she did get a second bag.

By now they were ready to start serving dinner. Mollie realized that just behind her a curtain had been pulled, separating the first class cabin from coach. She wondered what Karen, the woman from her Jewish dyke support group, was thinking. Mollie had run into Karen and her mother when the plane was boarding. They were sitting in coach, and knew there had been a mix-up with Mollie's seat, and that she was in first class. Shortly after take-off they had come up for a visit, to see what first class looked like. They were sitting in a non-smoking part of the coach, and Karen's mother was dying for a cigarette. Even though she didn't like sitting next to the smoke, Mollie enjoyed their visit. It made her feel a little less alone in that cabin. At the time, they had made jokes about Mollie's going to the Ritz; Karen's mother had said "Oy, fancy schmancy!" loudly enough for everyone to hear. Mollie had felt then that the other first class passengers had all looked to see who the loudmouths were. At the time, she had stared back brazenly. Now, she just felt cut off from the familiar; Karen and her mother were sitting on the other side of that stupid curtain.

Still, Mollie was comfortable, and she knew the food would be better here. The attendants began to come around with the trays for dinner. They were plastic trays, but big ones, and covered with cloth napkins to make a placemat. Mollie couldn't get her tray table up. It was in the arm of her seat, but she couldn't see any way to grab it and bring it up. The flight attendant, one of two WASPy looking men, leaned over to help her. Somehow he made her feel stupid for not seeing the little holder labeled "Pull" which brought the tray up out of the arm. He didn't say anything, but Mollie just knew he was thinking "If she weren't so fat she would have been able to see the Pull lever." It was a relief when the tray was up and this man stopped leaning over her. Mollie wondered if everyone but her in the cabin knew how to pull up their dinner tray.

The dinner trays were complete with glass dishes, cloth napkins and heavy silverware. The attendant came around with appetizers. Mollie was given a tiny ceramic bowl with cheddar cheese dip; the attendant then held out a tray with cut-up vegetables and tongs for Mollie to serve herself. She wondered how much she was supposed to take, and took less than what she really wanted. Then came a salad. While Mollie was eating her salad, rolls were carried around in a basket lined with yet another cloth napkin. But somehow the roll-carrying attendant managed to miss her, and Mollie didn't realize until she was almost finished eating. While Mollie was eating her salad, she overheard the attendant list "your choice of entrees" to one of the other passengers. Mollie decided she would have the filet mignon. First, though, she had a ridiculous conversation with herself.

> "It's probably not that good you know.
> I mean filet mignon on an airplane . . ."
> "How would you know good filet
> mignon from bad filet mignon —
> you've never had it in your life!"
> "I bet it's really small. It's one of those
> upper class foods that are supposed to be
> super delectable and are served in super
> tiny portions."
> "Well, stop and think a minute . . . you're
> not even really hungry anymore."
> "OK. OK, I'll try it. Who knows when
> I'll ever get another chance?"

But by the time the flight attendant got to Mollie, the filet mignon was gone, replaced in the list of entrees with lasagna. "Lasagna, for God's sake!" Mollie thought. She could get good lasagna for $4.45 right in the North End. She didn't have to think further, but went right to her second choice, duck in raspberry sauce. She had only had duck once in her life, and it was almost as big a treat as filet mignon.

While waiting for her main course, Mollie became painfully aware of the conversation in the cabin. At first, everybody but her seemed to be involved in that kind of cocktail party sociability rich people have. People were talking across the aisles to each other, and even the attendants were chatting with people as they delivered the dinners. Mollie continued reading while she ate her salad; for a minute she thought "If I weren't reading, I'd be in on it too." Then she remembered that this was an old fantasy — that she would fit in. If she stopped to think, even for a second, she knew she couldn't fit in with these people. She couldn't converse easily with them, and they certainly didn't want to talk with her either. She felt like she had stumbled into someone's fancy party.

When Mollie looked around, she saw that a few other people didn't seem to be in on the group conversation either. Even so, the whole atmosphere in the cabin was filled with a kind of easy chatter she could never make. Probably the free liquor didn't hurt, but Mollie knew she had never been that easy with strangers, even when she used to drink. "Especially all those men," she thought, "all so goyishe, all looking so rich." There was that kind of "men together" laughing in the air, rising under all other sound. It seemed very loud, and unbelievably jovial. For a minute, Mollie could hear nothing except that laughter.

When she stood up to go to the bathroom, she couldn't help comparing her old faded cotton shirt and jeans with the well-made, dressy clothes of the other passengers. She felt everyone stare at her as she walked to the front of the cabin. She was feeling "too fat" again, something which only happened when she was intimidated. In the bathroom, she tried to give herself a pep talk, about how being a dyke means being different, and about how she didn't really want to be like these people. She reminded herself about how gorgeous and strong she was *because* she was fat. Usually this worked, but Mollie felt only slightly better when she walked back to her seat.

Dinner was really good, though. Mollie read until she had to eat the duck and needed both hands to cut it. She put her book down, and cut and ate one piece at a time. This was, after all, the proper way to eat according to etiquette, and she was definitely on *their* turf now. While she ate, she thought about all the ways she wasn't like these people. She played her usual game of trying to figure out which things set her apart the most: being fat, being Jewish, being a dyke, looking dykey. Sometimes she thought that being working class didn't show to other people; right now she wasn't so sure. She wasn't paying attention to her food, and dropped a piece of duck from her fork to her chest. Fortunately, it fell into her V-neck, and didn't add yet another grease stain to her shirt. Mollie looked around to see if anyone had noticed, and was relieved that no one had.

"This place really has you jumpy," she thought. Usually she could get an attitude which made her feel better. But right now she just felt wrong: too big, too dykey, too Jewish, too poor, too . . . too everything.

The dessert tray had come and gone, and the flight attendant who followed it with a pot of coffee had forgotten to ask her if she wanted some. Mollie ate her dessert wishing she had some coffee to wash it down. She couldn't bring herself to call the flight attendant over to get a cup. She didn't understand why she couldn't and she felt even worse. She felt invisible, and a little trapped. She wondered how much longer this flight could last.

After dinner, after all the trays had been cleared and the cognac had been served, the flight attendants really got into visiting in the cabin. Not with her, but with everybody else. They seemed especially to enjoy the honeymooners, and the two jovial men sitting in the second row. By now, the honeymooners looked pretty drunk; they sat gazing into each other's eyes, giggling and kissing occasionally.

A well-dressed man, one of the jovial ones from the second row, came back to the flight attendant who was perched on the arm of the seat next to Mollie's, talking with the honeymooners. The man asked where he could smoke a cigarette. The flight attendant stood up, pointed to the seat next to Mollie's and said "Please sir, sit here. You can smoke in the last row of this cabin." The man lit up and sat down next to Mollie. While he smoked, he chatted with the honeymooners all about the beauty of his home state, Wyoming. He never once even looked in Mollie's direction.

After a few minutes, the young man in front of Mollie asked how much farther they had to go. She was happy to hear that it was almost time to land. The orange curtain, patterned to match the orange plush seats, was opened, and the thirteen people in first class were suddenly exposed to the hundreds in coach.

The thirteenth passenger, unplanned for and unwanted, was suddenly very glad. This flight was almost over. Next flight, maybe she wouldn't get so lucky.

Hot
Chicken Wings

JYL LYNN FELMAN

ESTHER WANTED SILENCE. It had been eight hours since she had met Channah and Saul in the Air Florida terminal, for their flight to Jamaica, and Esther was afraid she wasn't going to last the whole ten days. She had waited months for this reconciliation. But growing inside her was the terrible feeling that she needed to be saved from her very own parents. Then she laughed out loud. Maybe it was really Channah and Saul who needed to be saved from her, their very own daughter.

Esther took the elevator down to the lobby of the Windsor Hotel. Walking out the back door, she found herself in the middle of a pink patio. Hot pink lounge chairs were everywhere. Nothing was familiar. She was used to the Piccolo Porch, to all the Jews sitting in brown wicker chairs at the Doral Hotel in Miami Beach. But Channah said they should try some place new, different, to give the family another chance.

"Hello, darlin. Welcome to Ja'*mai* ca." Esther turned around, smack into Jamaica's face.

"Charlotte Gurthrie, here." Charlotte was smiling a

huge smile. Esther tried to smile back. She reached instead for the Jewish star hanging between her breasts.

"Esther Pearl Greenberg. I'm with my parents, we came here to talk." Charlotte wasn't just smiling. She was grinning from behind her eyes. But Esther could barely meet her smile, even though it was the smile itself she craved.

Charlotte was dressed in a uniform. A green military blouse covered her large round breasts. She wore a tight, khaki colored skirt, short above the knees, with black ankle socks and black tie shoes. "Are you the tour guide?"

"Girl, I guard I the doors right here at the Hotel Windsor." The woman was laughing in Esther's face.

Esther thought fast. She knew she couldn't spend all ten days with her parents, no matter how much she'd missed them over the last seven months. She took a deep breath. "I want to travel with you."

"By me, honey, it's okay. When ya want to see me *beau'* ti ful country?"

"As soon as possible, I mean it . . . and Charlotte," Esther swallowed hard before whispering into the big smile, "I go with girls."

"Girls be fine too, darlin." The guard reached out for Esther's hand. "Come by me, sweet darlin. I be waiting."

"Esther!" Channah walked out into the pink patio just as Esther's hand met the hand of the woman in the khaki colored skirt who was already turning around, walking towards the hotel lobby.

"Who was that?" Channah wanted to know.

"My tour guide."

"Esther Greenberg, you don't need a tour guide in Montego Bay. We came here for the sun. And to talk."

"I need a tour guide wherever I am." Esther needed patience. It had only been a year since she had told her parents the wonderful news that she loved women. "I'll meet you for dinner — just tell me what time." Esther understood her parents' disappointment. Not one of their three daughters had turned out according to the family plan. Her parents felt they deserved better than a divorce from a French Jew and a Freudian psychiatrist who didn't believe in standing under the *chupah*. The problem was that her parents didn't understand Esther's disappointment with them.

"Seven o'clock, sharp. We'll wait for you in the lobby." Esther tried to meet her mother's eyes; but when she did, all she saw was the flash of her mother's pain moving across her face. Esther wanted to hug Channah; to tell her she was glad they came to some place new. But she was afraid Channah wouldn't hug her back. Instead she nodded, turned around, and walked back into the hotel, wondering which door Charlotte was guarding now.

Esther stood alone in front of the elevators. When the doors opened, Charlotte walked out, almost bumping into Esther.

"Estie, where ya be keeping ya sweet self?" The gold in Charlotte's teeth caught her eyes.

"When does the tour begin?"

"Tomorrow's me off day." Charlotte's whole body smiled when she spoke. Her feet tapped the hotel floor lightly. Esther felt the smile coming up through the earth itself. By tapping her foot, Charlotte returned what she borrowed. "What's so busy in ya head, girl?"

"I was just watching you live." Esther winked at Charlotte. "So tomorrow's our day. What'll we do?"

"Whatever ya be wanting, sweet Estie. I be coming by early, us be having us the whole day."

"I want to eat Jamaican." Esther decided to take advantage of vacationing — for the first time in her life — beyond the brown wicker chairs of Miami Beach.

"Sure darlin, I be cooking. Wear ya walking shoes, girl. Us walking long to me house from the bus. Now this hotel here be needing a guard." After a quick nod goodbye, Charlotte walked away.

Alone in the elevator, Esther tried to understand what she wanted from this trip. She knew she had longed for her family. But she didn't miss the heartache that always followed being together as family, as Jews. Even studying at Brandeis where most of the students were Jews and she was majoring in Judaic Studies, hadn't brought back that warm feeling of belonging to her people. It was only Sunday. Esther told herself to take one day at a time, hour by hour if she had to.

At seven sharp Esther met her parents in the hotel lobby. They walked towards her just like two ordinary human beings. Everyone had dressed for the evening. Channah had on her favorite skirt-and-blouse ensemble. Esther had to admit her mother had good taste; the material was a soft silk, light blue and sea green. Channah's face was already tanned. Saul wore his summer suit, without a tie. He smiled at Esther.

"Where are we going for dinner?" Esther's voice was friendly.

"The Montego Bay Beach and Tennis Club, it's just up the road and comes highly recommended in the 'Kosher Traveller,' " Channah answered, not looking at Esther and not looking away, just looking.

Channah and Saul walked out the Windsor in front of Esther. They formed a perfect triangle. Esther remembered her therapist always said to stay away from triangles, only Esther had thought she meant love triangles, but now she knew that any triangle was dangerous, and that there was no way out, but physically to step out. Besides, a triangle was only half a Jewish star.

Saul asked the bellman to get a cab. Esther felt a large movement behind her. Charlotte.

"These folks ya parents, sweet darlin?" Esther reeled around, hostile, until she realized no one had heard the love talk but Esther and Charlotte. "Introduce me, if ya please . . ."

"These are my parents, Saul and Channah Greenberg."

"You're Esther's new friend, aren't you?" Channah said.

"Oh, Estie and me be knowing each other a very long time." Charlotte grinned. Esther didn't say a word.

"Cab's here," Saul called out. Charlotte walked with them.

For a minute Esther thought she was going to bend down and step right into the cab with her parents. But she didn't.

The cab pulled up at a giant ranch. As soon as they walked into the dining room, which was like an old cowboy movie — big round tables in huge circles circling a gigantic fireplace — Esther knew her mother was going to say that the dining room was a little too much. Saul looked around before making his announcement, "Not many of us in here."

"That's exactly what I was thinking." Channah looked at Esther for support. Esther knew her parents were uncomfortable in the strange *goyishe* dining room and so was she. For a moment, they were a family again.

But Esther couldn't stop thinking about Charlotte. Where was she? What was she having for dinner? Was she with her lover . . . Esther closed her eyes to see better: she felt the warmth of two big women sprawled out on a tiny double bed, feeding each other and laughing as the food spilled onto the sheets. Esther decided to have the fresh local tuna. She had read in *National Geographic* that it was a Jamaican fish.

She knew that tuna was kosher; the mothers didn't eat their young or prey off other fish. Esther had always hated the image of a mother eating her children. Whenever she smelled *treif* she immediately saw the floor of the ocean in her head. She pictured big shrimps, scallops, and giant oysters devouring their babies and any other fish swimming in their path.

Keeping kosher had always been important to Esther. When she was thirteen, right after her *Bat Mitzvah,* Esther had immersed herself in the meaning of *kashrut,* in hallowing the very act of eating. It was a way for Esther to eat with Jews everywhere and have Jews everywhere eat at her table.

She closed her eyes, wishing that she was alone with Charlotte. Esther hadn't remembered how depressing it was to be with her parents. She had always wanted an adult relationship with Saul and Channah. *Well, here it is,* she told herself. Then she had to put her fork down and stop eating. "I'm going to the bathroom, the waiter can take my plate."

She looked at herself in the mirror, shaking her head, not wanting to believe that absolutely nothing had changed. She knew her parents were unhappy. They had told no one, not even Rabbi Schwartz, that their baby wanted their blessing to bring home a Sabbath bride instead of a groom. So no one had brought up her life; no one had even asked her if she was happy.

Esther thought that being a lesbian made life with Channah and Saul so difficult. Her mother had stopped inviting her home for the holidays; and Saul had specifically said they weren't interested in any "details," not even Esther's new friends. She could still hear Channah's reaction to her good news: *But why did you have to go and spoil everything? Why tell us?* Esther knew then, that the only way into the Greenberg family was to be like Channah and Saul. There really wasn't anything to talk about. Esther returned to the table. She looked straight at her parents for the first time since arriving on the island. "I want dessert. Is anyone going to join me?"

"We'll split something with you," Channah said.

"No, I want my own." Esther shut her eyes and waited. Nothing happened. When the waiter came back she ordered Baked Alaska because she had always loved the taste of the meringue on her tongue as it melted.

Saul paid the bill while Esther took a last look at the big round tables. She was back at Camp *Ramah,* sitting with hundreds of young campers, cutting their kosher, *Shabbas* chicken breasts simultaneously. She stood to bless the wine, surrounded by over two hundred and fifty adolescent Jewish voices, singing as though their voices alone could call the prophet Elijah back to Earth. That was the last time Esther really felt at home.

Of course it never happened that the entire Camp *Ramah* dining room began eating at the exact same moment, but Esther used to fantasize every *Shabbas,* that all her people, everywhere, were striking matches as the sun set, welcoming in the weekly festival. In her mind for one brief moment, she had brought peace to the Jews, and to her family. Finally, Esther had to admit that being Jewish and being a Greenberg weren't the same thing.

"Estie, Estie!" Charlotte was waving her hands and calling to Esther. But it didn't look like Charlotte at all. Her green military blouse and khaki colored skirt were gone. Instead, she wore a purple beret balanced just above her left eyebrow. Deep red rouge was smoothed into brown skin; red lip gloss wet her mouth. Charlotte had hooped gold earrings, two and three, in each ear.

"Ya *finally* ready, girl?" Esther nodded, following her out the lobby of the Windsor Hotel and down the road to the bus stop. In the hot sun, Charlotte's black pants shined and her white blouse looked like silk. She carried a red and green, hand-woven pouch and a small, brown paper bag in her left hand.

Charlotte's legs moved fast on the gravel road. Esther had to run to keep up. This was a new Charlotte, quick, taking up space. On the bus, Charlotte sat down, stretched her legs out across an entire seat, and said hello whenever someone she knew walked by. Esther sat alone in the row directly behind Charlotte.

By the time they reached downtown, Charlotte was asleep and Esther's eyes were wide open. The bus stopped inside a huge open market decorated in banners of gold, green, shiny black and red. In booth after booth people sold food, clothes, records. The smells — red onions, ripe mango, dog shit — blended together, making Esther sick. Charlotte woke up, and motioned for Esther to follow.

They walked across the street to another bus stop, and waited ten minutes. They sat again in separate rows, as if they knew, without speaking that both of them needed a lot of space before their afternoon together. Pulling against the force of gravity the bus climbed straight up into the Jamaican hills, while the town below got smaller and smaller.

Skinny, bone-thin dogs ran everywhere; the driver kept his hand on the horn. A baby sat crying right in the middle of the road, sprawled out on all fours, trying to crawl to the other side. The bus circled around the screaming infant. As the bus climbed up, the temperature rose inside. Esther was hot. Everywhere there were trees, large wide-leafed palm trees reaching out, shielding the villages and the people.

Green, all shades; Jamaica was divided into shades of dark, light and yellow greens. From the window, the Jamaican green reminded Esther of Israel; slowly, she let in the yellow green Jamaican hillside. But she heard her father's voice in her head, like a tape recorded message playing over and over again: *Israel is the most beautiful country in the whole world.*

"Okay, Estie. Me stop is here." Charlotte hadn't spoken for at least twenty minutes; Esther didn't recognize her voice, but she felt them rise in unison, a pair of woman-bodies bending and rising together in dance. "Ready for some walking, girl?" Charlotte looked at Esther for the first time since

147

picking her up at the Windsor.

"What's in your bag?" Esther asked.

"Our supper, girl. I went I to the butcher this morning for the chicken, wings and legs." Charlotte was impatient. Esther didn't say a word; how could she explain the laws of *kashrut* to Charlotte?

Even though she wanted to eat Jamaican, she hadn't planned to eat *treif*. She never ate meat in restaurants unless it had been ritually slaughtered and blessed. Out of respect for her people, and for the food itself, Esther separated the kosher from the unkosher, the holy from the unholy, and ate only what was permitted by Jewish law. When she ate, Esther belonged to Jerusalem.

"Me kids be waiting . . . Estie, pick up your feet."

"Kids?"

"Oh yes, I has I three children, one boy and two female beauties, little ones, brown and beautiful." Esther didn't think she heard right; this was the first time Charlotte had said anything about kids.

"Charlotte, you got a husband?"

Charlotte nodded, her purple beret moved up and down. They walked side by side now; their buttocks moving from right to left, hitting each other slightly because they were walking up hill while their bodies pulled them down. "Me man he come and go; be working in Miami Beach most of the time. Send I a letter before he do home."

"What about your woman?" Esther concentrated on walking straight up hill. Charlotte didn't owe her any explanations.

"Oh ya darlin, whenever me man he be travelling, me girl Caroline and I, we goes to the bed and has us a sweet time. Sometimes us don't be up for a whole day, just to feed the kids and then us be meeting sweet again." They were almost at the top of the hill.

"Me man he love me, Estie. I got I he picture at me home. You'll see, girl." Charlotte pointed to a path off the dirt road. They headed straight down the side of the hill, into the overgrown weeds, bushes and very green palm trees.

Holding back a big yellow-green bush, Charlotte showed Esther where to walk. A slight odor came up to her nose; the same odor Esther smelled on her body whenever she was afraid. The path wasn't cleared well and the brush scratched her legs. They climbed down, deep into the underbrush; the deeper they went, the greener the leaves became, the stronger Esther's body smelled.

Looking up, she saw that Charlotte had taken them way off the main dirt road. They stood in the middle of a row of small wooden shacks. Walking over to the far end, they stopped in front of a silver tin door. Esther heard voices. Out of the bushes came a young boy as Charlotte whistled long and slow.

"Where are the beautiful ones?" Charlotte bent down to the size of her son, whispering and kissing inside each of his ears. "Are they with Caroline?" The boy nodded, standing almost at attention, watching Esther. His mother's eyes were in him.

"Let's go." Charlotte nodded towards the door.

The shack was a single room, as big as her Windsor closet and bathroom combined. In the center of the room was a double bed; Charlotte sat herself at the head. The boy jumped up, circling his mother with his body, protecting her. Esther stayed in the doorway.

To the right of the entrance was a big dresser with a mirror attached. Next to the dresser were several plastic milk cartons piled one on top of the other. From where she stood Esther could see dishes and silverware arranged in neat rows inside the milk cartons. On top of the cartons was a double gas burner. Everywhere, clothes were folded into neat piles.

149

The floor of Charlotte's house was made of firmly packed brown dirt. A broom was in the left corner by the doorway, and a dust pan. The only window was on the wall opposite the bed. The frame was empty, but the green from outside grew up around the glassless hole, filling it with a thick green softness.

"Estie, sit down, ya impolite girl; we in me own home now."

Charlotte cooked. She poured water from a jug on the floor into a sauce pan and added a cup of uncooked rice. She made a work space on the bed by propping up a six by twelve wooden board with two bricks at each end. Taking the chicken parts out of the bag she had carried since early that morning, she separated the legs from the wings, making two piles, dipping and rolling each piece into a flour mixture. After flouring each piece, Charlotte covered the chicken with spices. Esther watched, trying to figure out what the great rabbis would tell her about eating Charlotte's unclean food.

Charlotte lit the burner. She poured oil into a frying pan, waited a few minutes, watching the oil sizzle and get hot. Then one by one, she placed the wings into the hot pan, stopping for only a second to stir the rice. Every few minutes she added spices, red, black and green powders to the hot oil. When she was done frying the wings, she started over with the legs. Charlotte's love went straight into the frying pan and into the steaming rice.

On the bed, Charlotte spread out a single straw mat painted red, filled one plate with hot rice and fried chicken wings then put it on the mat in front of Esther. "Eat."

"I don't want to eat alone."

"Sweet darlin, where ya manners be? In Ja' *mai* ca the guest eats before the family. Eat."

Esther picked up the fork. What did it mean that she was about to eat Jamaican chicken wings and rice? She reminded herself that she had arranged this day, she had made the date with Charlotte and even told her she wanted to eat Jamaican. So Esther put some rice on the end of her fork, added a piece of chicken, and brought the fork slowly up to her mouth. She was eating Charlotte's wings, *treif* and unclean that they were.

The food had lost its heat, but when Esther put it in her mouth, she tasted all the Jamaican spices that Charlotte had added while she cooked. Spices Esther couldn't see by looking at the cooked food. She had to taste them to know that they were actually red hot and sweet all in the same bite. Like nothing she had ever tasted before.

Esther chewed. The spices were overpowering. This wasn't the first time that Esther had ever eaten *treif,* but in the past, whenever she brought unclean food to her lips, she had never been able to enjoy it as she did now. She remembered the first time she made love to a woman. That was the beginning. Esther had been afraid to bring her tongue down between Judith's legs. She had spent a long time kissing arms, shoulders, eyes, and face.

Finally there was nothing left to do but bring her wet tongue straight down Judith's breasts, stomach, and inside her thighs. Those first woman smells had been overpowering too, sweet and hot like Jamaican spices. When her tongue circled between Judith's small thighs, Esther told herself to open her eyes and look at the curly mound of dark, black hair protecting her lover's vagina, but she had been afraid to look.

"Tasting is the same as looking," Judith had said, reaching down to hold Esther's head close to her body. Esther had known she was right, so she let herself breathe in a little at a time, all the different smells hidden between Judith's legs. She remembered being surprised that the lips outside Judith's vagina had only a faint sweet smell. It was the inside that smelled strong and tasted so wet. Using her fingers to open

Judith, Esther had to fight off the pious old Jew in her head. He was tearing apart a red, *treif,* steaming lobster. Then slowly, as though praying, he dipped the white sweet, unholy fish into a pool of melted butter.

With her mouth inside Judith, Esther began to chew, taking small, gentle bites. Just as she was crossing over to join her lover, Channah and Saul pushed into her head. They stared at her, *their baby,* and Channah screamed, "Go! Wash yourself until you're clean, don't come into my house with any of that filthy *treif* still on your tongue. Get rid of the smell before you walk into my kitchen." Esther had had to stop, close her mouth before she gagged, and bring her head back up, next to Judith's.

They had held each other while Esther's whole body shook. But she wasn't shaking now. She was taking another bite out of Charlotte's sweet wing and thinking that all her life, she had been afraid of new, unknown, and different spices; but now, she was chewing bite by bite, Charlotte's crisp Jamaican skin.

"This is good. How do you get the flavors hot and sweet at the same time?" Esther piled more rice on her plate; stuffing her mouth full, she barely took time out to chew and swallow.

"Slow down, girl. Me knows ya had rice before. Ya eating like ya never ate in ya whole life." Charlotte shook her head; her son was laughing.

"I feel like I haven't eaten for days, even weeks." She was eating, really eating, almost as if for the first time. She laughed at herself. This then was Charlotte and Esther making love.

"Want to see some good pictures? I have I pictures of me, me man, and Caroline." Charlotte reached into another pile.

"Sure." Esther talked with her mouth full. They sat on

Charlotte's bed, her boy, Esther, and Charlotte looking at family pictures. They were in the livingroom now; Esther had finished eating and all the kitchen equipment had been pushed aside.

"This one me favorite, girl. Everybody I love and who love I be in here looking out at the world." Charlotte handed Esther a picture with three adults standing in the middle of the road. They held each other, looping their arms together behind their backs. Esther knew without asking who was in the picture.

"That's me woman Caroline, there on the end, me in the middle, and me man, Samuel on the other end." Esther stared at the picture. Something was going on in there that Charlotte wanted her to see.

"Ya done yet, with ya looking?"

Esther shook her head. Then she knew; it was in their bodies. If she looked closely at the way they stood, with their hips lightly touching and their thighs and knees bending into each other, Esther saw what Charlotte had been trying to tell her since they met. All three of them — Samuel, Charlotte and Caroline — were lovers. Esther steadied herself on the bed. She needed a few minutes to let in this new piece of truth, because it wasn't just about the three of them, living and loving in Montego Bay.

"So, you're all three together?"

Charlotte nodded.

"Anybody know besides me?"

"Impossible, sweet darlin. In Ja' *mai* ca a person gots to be either or, Estie, not both. They say there's not enough room in the world for us to be both. But I, girl, I hates to choose; I wants all there is. Ya the same, those hungry eyes, and that dancing mouth, told I right away. That's why me brought ya to me home. I been wanting someone from outside to talk to. So, I picked I sweet Estie." Charlotte reached for the picture.

"I girl, I separate in me own *beau* ti ful country. Me whole life, I be needing to tell somebody. Me opening doors, looking around, when I see ya coming into the Hotel Windsor. I knowing then, I found I somebody doing like I do."

So Charlotte was alone too, alone in green Jamaica. She had been eating unclean food, separate from her people, for years. Only she was doing just fine. It was Esther who had never learned that eating a little *treif* was necessary to survive.

Esther had never been free to eat whatever she wanted, because that meant eating alone, without the Jews. Esther had always been afraid to eat by herself; once she started she might never stop. There were too many things to taste, like Charlotte and Caroline and Samuel all at once.

"I've got to leave, Charlotte."

"I be waiting for ya to stand up, girl, saying ya had enough."

They looked at each other, closing out the boy, the hot chicken wings and rice, and the picture of Charlotte with her two lovers. Esther burned inside. This was only the second time in her whole life that she was full; the first time had been with Judith, her first woman lover. She had been unable to continue loving Judith like she wanted; every time she tried, she imagined her head turning into the red head of a steaming lobster whose antenna reached out to strangle her. But she didn't think that would happen anymore.

"I'll walk ya to the bus."

They walked then, back up the green path, past all the other shacks, and onto the road. When the bus came, Esther climbed the three steps by herself. In the center of the open market where all the smells blended together, Esther walked off the bus. She took a deep breath, slowly breathing in the pungent blend of dog shit, red onion, and ripe mango.

My Mother
Was a Light Housekeeper

THYME S. SIEGEL

HELLO, BERKELEY, your acid sparkled streets glistening through the smog, heartland in the production of rhetoric, land of free boxes, neighborhood warning systems, block dances, food conspiracies, and my relatives. Aunt Riba and Uncle Roy's bright one-story stucco, catty-corner to a decaying mansion — where some of their children live communally.

Rosh Hashonah. I wonder why Jewish New Year begins in the fall instead of the spring. The spring would feel more natural. I reach their doorbell just as Mom and Dad drive up in their camper. Everyone on time for the holiday dinner. Me, Mom and Dad have never been here before because Aunt, Uncle, and Sarah, the Old Mother, have just moved to Berkeley to be near their children. Everyone very keyed up. Riba, Roy, and Sarah all answer the door. Excited talking, sharing information about missing members of the clan. Showing family photos. I drift to the rear and notice Sarah, the Old Mother, standing at the doorway to the back porch.

"We had a nice house in D.C.," Sarah says to me in familiar yet surprising Yiddish accents, a sound I have not heard for years. She is very short and stooped, wrinkled, not older but ancient. "It had a lot of room, big backyard, lots of flowers and trees." I can see into the backyard here: tiny.

"Yes, but they left that house and moved here?"

"They wanted to be near the children."

"Your great-grandchildren."

"Yes, them especially, Lillakah and Lil'Umbillakah."

I look wonderingly at the Old Mother, a fantastic survivor. A Ukrainian. She is so short it is easy to overlook her wrinkled face. But I look at her carefully. I had overlooked my own grandmother.

"You knew my Bubie?" (I ask after my grandmother.)

"Yes," Sarah whispers. "A very progressive woman, very progressive. I knew her in Elsinore, when I lived in Los Angeles." The rest of the family is floating towards us. I see Mom's attention about to catch onto our conversation. I tighten up and respond quickly, "Yes! I was there too."

"Elsinore is a Yiddishe shtetl," Sarah comments.

"Yes, I know," I whisper quickly, as Mom interjects. "Yiddishe shtetl! She doesn't know what you mean, grandma, these kids don't know what it means —" Ha ha ha ha, they laugh about how these kids don't understand.

"I know what it means," I say, but she and Sarah are talking away in Yiddish. (Oy Gottenyu, she's auf tsurus. A Shaynim Donk in Pupik.) It is true I don't understand much.

"It means Jewish ghetto," Mom stops long enough to tell me.

"I *know.*"

"Well, that's better than the rest of these kids."

"You only spoke Yiddish to each other, not to us." You and Dad spoke in your thick private flavors. We were outside of it; we spoke English in harsh unhappy tones, coping with public school in rural America . . . "But I *was* in Elsinore and I'm *not* a total idiot."

Mom blue-eyes me, smiling. Is it OK to come out with

it like that? Did I hurt her? A record in Hebrew I never heard before is playing on the stereo. "Anachnu Ve'Atem" is the refrain, a powerful chant from Israel.

"What's that, Mom?"

"A song about Us and Them."

I don't know how to ask Mom if I have hurt her. It is very beautiful music so it catches us for awhile, then she wanders off to join a conversation with my aunt, who is setting the table. I turn back to the Old Mother. "I know Elsinore is the West Coast shtetl. I could easily see that. The only ones in the streets and the stores are elderly Jews."

"Yes, and they have a community center," says Sarah.

"Yes, I know. Bubie and I went there. To a concert. A woman was singing in an evening gown. Bubie started singing too."

"Yes, she loved to sing. Such a good voice too."

"The people who were running the show didn't think she should sing because it wasn't her concert. A man came over and told her to stop singing. She got really pissed off. We had to leave. She was mad and didn't want to stay anymore. As we walked out, she muttered resentful curses at the people who ran the community center, all the way out, real loud, everyone heard and turned around as we left."

"She was an individual, very stubborn, very progressive."

The dinner table is covered with white paper, centered with candelabra, and dotted with red wine bottles. For a moment I recall the ancient ceremonies, chanting in Hebrew for three hours around the table before we could eat, the ancient ceremonies during which I stared at the matzoh crumbs and the red wine stains on the white paper. While the grandfather chanted in a language I didn't learn, and all the relatives jabbered away in yet another language I did not learn. What does anything mean? I long ago tired of asking, or maybe I never did ask. I am a foreigner in the ancient culture,

157

the languages, the traditions. I am light years away. Or has it only been a generation? In me, the tradition of five thousand years dies. I am the daughter who cannot carry on the family name, practice the ceremonies. I am the daughter who searches for a new tribe. Who searches for primitive solidarity in a new culture of women. What was coherent for them has never been coherent for me.

"Maybe you'd want to write a book review for *Freiheit?*" asks Uncle Roy. (*Freiheit* is a socialist journal which he edits, modeled after the old *Freiheit*.)

"No," I say, flatly and glumly. "I've done that already. Book reviews are fine, but first I want a different space."

"She doesn't want to do journalism anymore, Roy." Aunt Riba. I look at her in surprised gratitude.

"What do you want to write? For whom? To be published in a book? Magazine, where?" Uncle Roy demands.

"A book maybe."

"What, a novel, fiction, what?"

"Something which emanates from the dream consciousness. *Freedom begins in the realm of dreams,*" I quote.

"Freedom is only in the realm of dreams," says Sarah, in Yiddish. Mom translates to the rest of us, the younger generation.

A silence follows. Then Uncle Roy continues dominating the dinner conversation with social, political issues. Mom, Dad, and Aunt Riba follow along avidly while the rest of us red-diaper babies, in various stages of dress and stress, delicately slurp and gobble the split pea soup, chicken, and mushrooms.

"Do you think the working class is becoming more progressive?" asks Uncle Roy of my father.

Dad clears his throat. "Well, I can tell you, from traveling around the country a lot and living in trailer parks these last several years, I can tell you they are still very reactionary," says Dad, in his slow laryngitic voice.

"Or maybe it's the union leaders who are," adds Mom.

Why is it that I am always surrounded by people speculating on the working class — is it capable of transforming itself in the U.S.? Can there be a revolution? I am still in the heartland of theory, with my relatives. I haven't seen Mom and Dad in a year; we've all been traveling around. I want to talk about experiences.

"Who have you met lately? Who travels in these trailers?"

"We met some travelers in Montana who used to live down the road from us," says Mom.

"Really, who?"

"Oh, we never knew them when we lived there. They were on their way to moving to Grants Pass, Oregon. . . . *We* could never move to Grants Pass," Mom ends sharply.

"Why not?" I ask, still not getting it.

"Because we're Jews." (Get it, get it?)

"I can't just move anywhere I want either," I say. "I mean lesbians can't." Mom looks at me, somewhat pained.

"Isn't that where you spent the summer, Cheike, around there? At a festival?" Dad.

"What kind of festival?" asks Uncle Roy, perking up.

"A women's spiritual gathering."

"What's that?" he persists.

"Ummm, uh, uhmmm," I look around the table. Everyone is staring down at their chicken, listening intently. What to say? "It was women getting together on land, like a campout, to center ourselves as a group. We're developing our own culture." Unfortunately, I get into it and go on. "But we didn't own the land, and the man who owned the land insisted on being there."

"You've gone too far," says Dad. "Why do you have to have all-women gatherings and always say, 'Too bad there was a man there'? It's like colored people when they got money at first they went out and bought Cadillacs but now some of 'em drive VW's."

I can't follow the logic of Dad's remark so I turn to my aunt and Mom, who are sitting together, seeming to agree with Dad. "You have to experience working with all women and being with all women. You've been married for decades and decades, how would you know?"

"Oh, I have experience," answers Mom, with a touch of hauteur.

"The women at B'nai B'rith used to get together every week," adds Aunt Riba.

"It's not the same thing. You went home to husbands afterwards. Living with men and visiting or going to meetings is different than living with all women . . ."

At this point my uncle gets up, grandiosely announcing that he will wash the dishes.

"I'm going to help him," says Mom, with laughing emphasis.

"How long can a group of women stay together?" asks Dad. "It's not like you have kids to keep you together."

I move my mouth to protest. Some lesbians have kids. Why do you need kids to stay together? What does stay-together mean? How important is it? But how can I ask them? *They* don't know.

"Women living just with women, ay meshugge," continues Dad. "It's absurd." Almost everyone laughs, thinking of the absurdity of it. Not maliciously, though, it is just ludicrous to them. Nothing I say can make it real; I don't have the answers, the experiences, five thousand years of ritual at my fingertips, five thousand years of red wine at my lips, to make them speak the words from beyond the heartland of rhetoric. I try to imagine my tribe, we who will shout *KinsWoman!* to each other in a tribal tongue. I imagine us in a dance to the light, our own festival of light, into ourselves and into each other, dancing around candles on the Solstice. I imagine saying to the children, "We have danced this dance and chanted this chant for five thousand years. It celebrates the eternal return of the light."

These are the words, but I do not have them.

Walking along the streets of the colonial town where I went to high school, I am with a very open being. A being who has just come into the country from Nepal or Ceylon. But I sense she is the same one from high school, the mysterious Sing, who appeared those years to us in stately silence, elegant, impeccable Sing, forever the profile of the kiss not taken. I am showing her Main Street.

Then the scene shifts to the farm: Nuovev Jasmine. She has a room under our roof, like a nest in the eaves. We go up to my little bedroom overlooking the pond, right under her nest. As we lie in bed together, we can see the sun rising over the trees around the pond. We are touching, I am touching her face, so tender and clear. She is open to me.

I ask her questions. I take off the last of my clothes and then she does too, smiling, watching me. The softness of her caress across my breast is like silky seaweed on underwater skin. Everywhere I am opened, sensual.

Suddenly, the sense of another. Vashti is sitting hidden in the blankets at the foot of the bed, staring at the sunrise. My younger sister. I feel around the blankets. "So there you are. Why don't you open the downstairs drapes?" (Same view.)

"That's OK, I'm going outside," she says, and goes. I lie back. We're spending the whole day in bed together, timelessly. "I don't know what time it is because I don't have any clocks around," I explain, although it is not necessary. Then the dream changes, turns round. I'm waking up.

*

Cheike! Cheike! "Are you ready to face reality?" asks my mother, with her own brand of gentle sarcasm. The fragile film of the dream is dissolving. Oh, what was it? The feeling of spending the whole day in bed with a woman, a very large woman who holds me, with long, thick red-gold hair. And cascading matzoh boxes at the very end.

Daylight streams into the trailer. Mom turns on the nine o'clock news. Patty Hearst capture news. Reality. I am not lying with my lover. I have no lover. I am with Mom and Dad in their trailer. California sunshine is bouncing off all the cement and metal in this trailer court.

"Can I turn off the radio?" I leap up, turning off the radio.

"Don't you want to hear what's really happening in the world?"

"I can't do anything to help Patty Hearst. I want to write in my journal."

Mom is washing the dishes, standing firmly in sneakers and anklets. She glances over at the marbled cardboard notebook I open, like the ones from grade school. Back on the farm, it hadn't occurred to me to write in front of anyone, and I had never seen anyone else write. It was a deep dark secret, like what happened behind closed doors in bathrooms and bedrooms.

"Do you ever read it, or do you just write in it?" Mom asks.

"No read, just write, ha ha ha." No, I don't show my writing. What if I opened my books to Mom and Dad, showed my whole self, dark green and silent childhood? But my flippant manner has closed the subject.

"Yes, I reread it sometimes. I learn from it." Whoever wrote in a journal on the farm? All I ever saw was a locked wooden box of Mom and Dad's love letters. And my older sister's locked diary, in which she vowed never to tell a future husband she had lost her chastity. Nuovev Jasmine, a paradisi-acal Jewish chicken farm in the forties and fifties, when adventuring into the interior was called "too subjective." Politics and economics were going to save the era. And politics was what got you in trouble and made people hate you. The childhood faces of the Rosenberg boys haunted my childhood from the back cover of *DeathHouse Letters*. Which sat on their dresser for years, like a permanent fixture. I recall that bedroom, which looked out over the pond. The double bed I had to cover so precisely — but never lie on. The night table next to it on Mom's side, upon which sat *The Well of Loneliness* (in paper) and a lamp, also for years.

"Why don't we ever share what it felt like to live at Nuovev Jasmine?"

Mom looks at me warily. I used to be so critical of her. She finishes drying her hands on a dish towel. "What do you want to talk about?"

I feel shaky, on thin ice, but ready to skate — "I hear you calling my name. Like a shattering reverberation over fifty acres of corn stubbles, rattling through the woods. 'Cheikkkkeeeeeeee . . .'

"It is winter, the corn stubbles are frozen, my feet crunch in the snow. I want to explore how the eastern woods look in the snow, the density, the designs, the feeling of the snow transforming an already secret place. It was not a place where anyone accompanied me. I could see Dad driving the pick-up on a far western cornfield, heading toward the gar-bage pit. You were calling from the porch, you wanted me to help with the laundry . . ." Mom's tan face is frowning.

Is it OK to talk like this? Dad is outside the trailer, I can see him setting up a vise-grip on the back of the camper, his new workroom. A condensation of the garage and feedroom at Nuovev Jasmine. I can see his white hair curling up the back of his neck as he bends forward in concentration. He is making earrings out of nickels. Mom gets up to sweep the floor, commenting that what she does and what Dad does is what is most comfortable for each. There is no problem. As she moves around, the trailer shakes, the floor shakes, and the ceiling shakes. Reminding me of dawn. (At dawn the rocking trailer woke Mom up. "What's going on?" she asked in a startled urgent voice. From my berth I stopped wiggling and didn't tell her what was going on. Just laughed that I had had a farm dream again.)

"So what? I was doing the laundry . . . Dad was dumping the garbage, you were —"

"What? What was I?"

Mom's eyes light up to answer, "I didn't want you to do the laundry, Cheike. Actually, I wanted you to do the eggs!"

"Ah yes, you wanted me to do the eggs. Remember when the bouncing trailer woke us this morning? I was having a dream of packing eggs!" (I still won't say I was masturbating.) "I was bouncing in my dream." At this point Dad comes in and leans against the door frame, listening to us. "Only I'm not packing eggs for Nuovev Jasmine, I'm packing eggs for *Amazonia*. It's clearly printed in blue on the side of each thirty-dozen box. The eggs are all packed strangely, all different sizes — jumbos and peewees together, checked and cracked, flats and fillers not filled to the proper amounts . . ."

We all laugh. Yea, the egg room, grading and packing all those years, a fragile egg myself, thin and unexposed, not like those hardy egos developing in the outside world. Eggs falling off the machine and smashing on the cement — eaten by wild chicken-coop cats, darting in at the sound — eggs crunched together on the way from the washer to the grader, squeezed and falling, eggs outside crunched by tractor tires, eggshells in the mud. Huge white eggs and little inverts, soft-shelled eggs, malleable in fingers, floppy, lacking — calcium? Lacking the right support . . . The Large go in the large, the Mediums go in the medium, the Pullets go in the pullet. . . Experiences rolling down the blue runways of the grader table, and you pack them away fast; so they don't pile up, and ship them in caseloads to the Cities . . .

But the soft ones, maybe they didn't smash as hard and fast as the firm ones. Eggshells in Amazonia, which exists in our northwoods minds like an Atlantis on land. Like the new continent of Mu. The trick is to reach Amazonia without these old, almost fatal wounds. Might this trailer understand Amazonia — understand it as the total space, separate culture, the earth and sky. And eggs, Mom and Dad understood: eggs, seeds, and ponds.

"I want to ask you something, Cheike." Mom, in a serious tone. Oh, no! What is it? "Why did you change your name?"

Reflex: defense. "Because these Anglos can't pronounce Cheike properly."

"It doesn't make sense to me. People will mispronounce your new name too."

"It's a tribal name. I belong to a different tribe now. But I have many names. To you I am still Cheike."

"To me, you are still Baby." She laughs. I don't mind her laugh, but I bring her up to date. "I'm not a baby anymore though, you know, I'm a lesbian woman . . ."

"Why do you always have to bring up being a lesbian?"

"I hardly ever do — that you hear."

"Like last night."

"Because it fit in. You always think you're different and can't fit in anywhere in small town America, and that's true, but there are lots of reasons why people don't fit in and can't move anywhere they like. It goes double for me. There are very few places I can live. You wonder why I don't settle down, and that's why. I have to find a women's community I can live in . . ." I look up at Dad, who is shaking his head. "What, no?"

"Tell me, Cheike," his old hoarse voice, "do you have to be a lesbian to be a feminist?"

Oh no, that question again. I can pretend I don't know. "I don't know. I did — have to become a lesbian before I could be anything but a feminist literary critic. But that was because my ideas were years ahead of my behavior. Some of my ideas."

"Don't you think women can oppress other women?" pursues Dad. "I know some very domineering women."

"Yea, sure. The difference is in a group awareness. Now we try to avoid the roles that reinforce oppression."

"That's you and your friends. There are domineering women."

"I'm talking about what lesbians all over the country are trying to do these days. . . . Let's go to the beach!" I say in sudden inspiration, my fingers almost burning against the hot silver metal outside the open door.

It is our last day together. Mom and Dad are heading for Arizona in their trailer and I to Oregon in my VW bug. Everyone agrees to the trip to the beach. We do not rush.

"Tell me, what are you going to do from here? Are you going to settle down?" Mom continues.

"You sound like Bubie."

"We're worried about you."

"I see my life as a story: at first I was very threatened. I escaped by running into the pond and going underwater. I held out for a long time, long enough, although once when I did pop up I got shot at. I went under again — long enough to be in a later age, a different time and place. I come up. It feels quiet now, safe now. I go to a house where I feel attracted; a woman is there I want to see. To leave, we have to climb out the second story window down an escape, because of her husband, who wants to continue to possess her. But I want to leave, and she follows me. We go out on a road, which is a ledge, a narrow ledge of ourselves. To the right is an enormous drop; to our left, a sheer cliff wall. We are following the path to Amazonia."

"Where's Amazonia?"

"It's an erotic hillside in Brazil. It's a scenario."

"A scenery? A Brazil scenery?"

"Huh. It's women, all kinds of women, egg women, crying young egg girls growing up in so many shapes and sizes, checked and cracked, who grew up in so many conditions but together at last. Not sorted out into hierarchies, you might say . . . or I might say, anyway . . . anarchy and variety are our beginning characteristics."

Silence. Then, "Your generation has had a much better opportunity to associate with each other from different social, religious, and economic backgrounds." Wow! She understands. "Then there's psychological backgrounds and astrological backgrounds . . . !" I have to add.

"Let's go."

On the way we stop to pick up Daro, a young woman who wants a ride with me to Oregon. May as well start early. Although I don't know Daro at this point, I know that with her along I won't be outnumbered. I associate her as one on my path.

Daro smiles calmly and swings in the front seat of my bug. Mom and Dad are in back. Her vibrant brown eyes beam familiarity.

"Why do women wear beards these days?" asks Dad. Oh no, he has noticed Daro's strong stray chin hairs. Daro looks at me suddenly and then turns around to the back seat. "Why don't you?"

Mom comes in here, rendering a textbook lecture on

hormonal balances in each sex. She remembers a dark-haired girlfriend from high school who had had chin hair. I glance over at Daro's shoulder, covered with glistening reddish-dark hair. "Was that the one who didn't want you to get married, Mom?" I pipe up. "Yes, that was the one."

"It's defiance," says Dad. Dad still believes in some of the hierarchies of family and society.

"Defiance! It takes courage to be ourselves in a society with its overpowering demands for a certain look!"

Mom agrees. Dad goes on, "You'd be safer on the streets if your appearance conformed. That's why the Jews got away from wearing payess, yarmulkahs, and black robes. Why do you think? I see some women walking around in ripped, dirty jeans. People aren't tolerant. They'll attack you if you look different."

I can tell Dad is recalling his boyhood in eastern Poland. He knows what it is like to be hated because of how you look. He is trying to warn us compassionately, but I am pretty sure he is offending Daro, who stares down at her velvet jeans patches.

"How you look is not reason for men to attack women," says Mom.

"Yes, but it makes you stand out, that's when people attack you, when they think you hate them."

"We're into love, not hate, Dad."

"The world isn't ready for love."

I stare out along the gorgeous coastline. What is the world ready for, then?

"Let's pull over," I say, and I pick a beach, a pull-in near an artichoke field. Beyond that, there is a promontory with a lighthouse on the end.

"Can you pick any beach?" "Yes," I assure them, "that is what I always do." They have not been to a Pacific beach before. Daro bounds out over the dunes as soon as we stop.

Mom and Dad settle face down on a blanket. Dad goes to sleep, and Mom reads a *Country Women* magazine I gave her. She unzips the back of her sundress. Only the skin around her neck is freckled and tan. Dad's whole back is dark-red bronze, like their faces. The contrast with their white hair strikes me. Mom's blue eyes sparkle out to me. Together with them at last on a Pacific beach, we are a flock of water-sharers. No one else is on the beach, just us refugees from the East — and Daro. Here the ocean is not blocked into swimming areas like the Middle Atlantic, no boardwalks, no saltwater taffy stands, no screaming rides. Just dunes, wildflowers, cliff walls, spun sponge rocks, phosphorescent caves. A freshwater stream — flowing through a crater of sand nearby. Around us — trails of seagull feathers and transparent sacs of jelly.

Daro reappears, examining the purple sac inside one, a glob of jellyfish, watching the bubbles blow within it. She hands me a feather and sinks down on the blanket, resting her hand on my knee. Mom on my other side reaches her hand around me to touch Daro. Her hand doesn't quite reach so she wiggles around and moves up an inch so she can reach. Daro's self-absorption is like soft tissue wrapped around a sharp object. Mom wants to make up for the car conversation. Dad decides to tell a joke. "Once there was a kid who dared her father to eat half a worm: 'I'll eat half if you eat half.' The father takes up the dare and eats half the worm. He gives the other half to the kid, but the kid says, 'You ate the wrong half!'" Daro likes this story and laughs, bowing her head over my lap, laughing.

"I didn't mean anything before about how you look, honey, I was just talking." Dad's laryngitic kindly voice. He has a cold. Daro looks at him and relaxes. He is a grandfather, and tired, smiling inside his thinning curly mop of white hair, his red skin criss-crossed with lines.

"Mom and Dad used to be farmers, Daro, now they are

gypsies, like us." I want her to know them, to feel safe and accepted with them, as I do, because I feel how suspicious she is of parents. Later, I discover she is more like them than I will ever be. Those three are of the earth, and I am of the air. For years I resisted Mom and Dad, not just their parental intonations, but as representatives of the material plane itself. The maintenance of a real farm. They had long ago freely admitted to not being philosopher-poets — my one requirement for the people I live with — but bread-and-butter folks, the people who keep the home front repaired. I was a little Rimbaud monster hatched from the cosmic egg, seeking visions. Later, I learned that air needs the protection of earth, and the earth needs the air to breathe. We unite in the sight of the water and the fire. It would be neat to stay and have a camp fire on the beach.

"I wish I hadn't felt so separated from you two for so long. We could have shared a lot more."

"You wouldn't unlock your door," says Mom.

"You didn't ask the right questions."

"We didn't realize you felt separated. Parents assume they can tell what's going on, they don't ask questions," says Dad.

"Your father didn't converse with you, draw you out, did he, Dad?" Dad exhales sharply, like *Are you kidding?* His father was a rabbi from the Old Country, not attentive to the psychology of childhood.

"You know," says Mom, "my mother always asked a lot of questions and I resented it. I kept my distance from you. I didn't want to intrude like that."

"Oh, I'm a bird, I love like a bird," I say. What is the use of going over the past, the years I spent behind a closed door, a little alcove where I wrote things I never admitted to and gazed at the pond from my attic window. "I was a bird, trapped in an attic." I laugh. And then lapse into broody silence. Daro smiles brightly sparkling brown eyes at me and reaches around, tentatively touching my shoulder. I reach around Mom and knead her shoulders. Smooth the little knots. Imagine she is doing the same to me. Dad goes back to sleep. I concentrate on breathing in and out. Mom looks over the *Country Women* magazine I gave her, an issue on "older women." After awhile she says, "What about older men? I don't want to leave my boyfriend." And puts her arm around Dad's sleeping form. I don't know; I don't know. My eyes feel tired, either from the sun or from uncried tears. *When* am I going to be wherever I should be? And they, who have each other only, where can they settle down, their new Jerusalem? Not in the same direction as Amazonia. We are cultural refugees together for only a few weeks each year, on our separate roads. Nuovev Jasmine is gone, the pond a swamp again. I haven't been back, but I saw that in a dream. Never again can we skinny-dip, boat, or skate on it. The pond is shrunk and dirty, receded from the pier, ukky. The man who bought it turned it into a sewage disposal for his trailer park.

I jump up, facing the vast expanse before us. I want to swim; I rip off my clothes and run down into the tide. Raising my arms high and jumping, a tremendous wave crests beneath me. There is only the Adventure left, only the quest for a new native land. Look at them on the shore, here for only one moment do we inhabit the same reality, here at land's end, Mom, Dad, Daro and me in the same shot, the same frame. Click!

Over the dunes a man in street dress appears. He says, "This isn't a public beach, it's my beach." So we have to leave here. Dad wants to go anyway, he's not feeling that well. I slip into my soft gym pants, but the waist drawstring is lost down its slot. I feel tired, I want to flop down, not leave. I feel like a baby, wanting to cry in frustration because I can't get the string to come through the slot. To scream and cry like a baby.

"Mom . . . ?"

"You do it with a safety pin. Here." She stands in front of me, patiently threading the knot through the opening. I stand silently watching, like a pacified toddler. I can see the lighthouse behind her, at the edge of the promontory. Victorious, finished, she stands straight and smiles. Sardonically, she says, "Your mother is a light housekeeper . . ."

Virgo woman, steadiness and continuation in seas of change, *I salute you.*

Glossary

anachnu ve'atem - We and you (plural). Us and them.

Ashkenazim - Jews of German and Eastern European descent.

bat mitzvah - The age at which a Jewish girl attains religious maturity (twelve years and a day). Also, the celebration and ceremony.

bubbe (bobbe, bubie) - Grandmother.

bubbe meiseh - Grandmother's tale; old wive's tale, tall tale, nonsense story.

bubeleh - Little grandmother; used as a term of endearment for a girl child.

Chanukah (Hanukkah) - Festival of Lights, lasting eight days, commemorating the rededication of the Temple in Jerusalem.

chumetz - Leavened food. Just before Passover, orthodox Jewish women clean their houses thoroughly, after which there is a ritual where the house is swept with a feather to get any stray crumbs of chumetz that may remain.

chupah - Marriage canopy.

daven - To pray.

dreck - Garbage.

dybbuk - The soul of a dead person which enters and controls the body of a living person.

fershimmeled - Confused.

gentile - A person who is not Jewish.

glesele - A glass.

goyishe - Characteristics of non-Jews.

Hassid (Chassid) - Adherent of Hassidism, a religious movement founded by the Baal Shem Tov.

ima - Mother.

kashrut - The set of dietary laws which govern eating habits.

kinder - Children.

kosher - Food that is permitted and prepared according to Jewish dietary laws.

matzoh (matzah, matza, matzo) - Unleavened bread, made chiefly for Passover.

maydeles - Young girls.

mazel tov - Congratulations, good luck.

meshugge, meshuggeneh - Crazy; crazy person.

midrash - Interpretations of the Bible in story form.

minyon - The quorum of ten men required to have a Jewish service.

mishegoss - Craziness.

mishpuchah - Family.

mitzvah - Blessing.

motzi - Blessing over the challah on Sabbath.

nu - [A question is implied] So? Well?

oi, shi'madele - Oh my pretty girl.

oy Gottenyu - Oh my God.

oy vey - An expression of surprise, sadness, fear, etc.

payess (peyes) - Side curls worn by very observant Jewish men.

Purim - Holiday celebrating the saving of the Persian Jews from massacre.

Rosh Hashonah - Jewish New Year.

schlep - Pull, drag.

seder - Traditional meal eaten on the first two nights of Passover.

shabbas (shabat, shabes) - Sabbath

Shavuos (Shavout, Shevouth) - Festival celebrating the success of the spring growing season.

shiksa - A non-Jewish woman (often meant as a pejorative).

shlemiel - A clumsy or foolish person.

Talmud - Body of literature interpreting the Torah.

tante - Aunt.

tefillim - Phylactaries containing scriptural quotations, worn on the forehead and left arm by Jewish men during weekday morning prayers.

treif - Not kosher.

vas - [A question is implied] What?

vey is mir - Woe is me.

yarmulkah (yarmulke) - Traditional skull cap worn by Jewish men.

Yom Kippur - Day of Atonement; a solemn day of fasting and repentance.

zhlub - Slob.

zi g'zunt - Be well.

Contributors' Notes

MARCY ALANCRAIG: I am a native Californian who grew up in a "free-thinking" and non-religious household in Christian suburbia. My "coming out" as a Jew was harder on my atheist parents than my coming out as a lesbian. I live with Paula Ross, my lover of ten years, in a bi-racial, bi-cultural household that celebrates diversity, cats, home-cooking and the complexity of life in earthquake country.

I am currently working on a novel called *Hatching Ground*, about Jewish chicken farmers of Petaluma, California. This gives me the opportunity to weave together stories from my Ashekazi European heritage along with stories about the rural California hills I love so much.

ELANA DYKEWOMON: What it means for me to be a lesbian and a Jew permeates my work. I live in Oakland among Jewish dykes whom I love, and whose love for me makes a hammock in which I can rest, dream and survive earthquakes. I typeset to pay the rent. I am the current editor of *Sinister Wisdom*, a journal for the lesbian imagination in the arts and politics.

I am the author of *Riverfinger Women, They Will Know Me By My Teeth* and *Fragments from Lesbos*. I have published essays, fiction and poetry in *Nice Jewish Girls: A Lesbian Anthology; Shadow on a Tightrope: Writings by Women on Fat Oppression; The Tribe of Dina: A Jewish Women's Anthology; Naming the Waves: A Lesbian Poetry Anthology,* and *For Lesbians Only: A Separatist Anthology.* I am part of the tape *Dyke Proud,* a lesbian poetry reading from the 3rd International Feminist Bookfair in Montreal, 1988, and I have published in many journals, including *Common Lives/Lesbian Lives* and *Sinister Wisdom*.

JYL LYNN FELMAN: My identity as a Jew and as a lesbian is not static; I am in perpetual negotiation with myself and others. I struggle for lesbian visibility within the Jewish community and Jewish visibility in the radical gay, feminist and leftist communities. To be truly myself means to confront the enormous homophobia in the mainstream Jewish community while at the same time, longing to celebrate, to be welcomed as *mishpuchah*, by those same Jews. To be truly myself means also to confront the huge ignorance about Jews — Jewish culture, history, language and customs — among radical feminists who are on the cutting edge of every other political issue. Today, in those places I call home, I live with contradiction — living fully without full recognition of who I am. I long to tell all my stories, to swallow my censors forever, and to liberate my lesbian Jewish imagination.

My work has been published in the following journals: *Genesis 2, Sojourner, Tikkun, Penumbra, The Syracuse Review* and *Korone*. I have had stories published in *The Tribe of Dina: A Jewish Women's Anthology* and *Word of Mouth: Short-Short Stories by Women*. I have recently completed a short story collection, *Hot Chicken Wings*.

JUDY FREESPIRIT: I've always been a Jew. Born in Detroit, Michigan in 1936, I grew up during WWII, the daughter of two first-generation Americans. My Jewish cultural identity is strong, though I am not religious. I recognize my Yiddish-speaking ancestors in some of my speech patterns. I like this and feel proud of the history of resilience and determination of my people. I feel connected with my Ashkenazic Jewish heritage and identify strongly with its symbols, traditional foods and music, as well as with its ethical and social values.

I became a lesbian when I was thirty-something. Just about the same time I also became a feminist and fat activist. In those early days of budding new consciousness there wasn't enough time to do justice to any one of my identities, much less all of them, so I spent most of my time on lesbian/feminist politics, with a smattering of fat work wedged in where I was able. My Jewishness didn't seem to be an issue at that point. Later I became disabled, which left me with an additional identity which required additional energy output at a time when I had less energy to put out. Exhausted, I stopped political activity for several years as I worked on healing. It was during this period that I came to realize how all of my identities wove a pattern in my life. As I began to heal physically I also began to mend the tears in the fabric of my identity. The tool I used was writing. Now I am 53 years old and no longer see myself as just a Jew, nor just a lesbian, nor just fat. I am the unique combination of my own genetic, psychological, social and cultural identities — like a unique patchwork quilt. I like that image. It covers a lot.

My writing has appeared in several anthologies, including: *Shadow on a Tightrope: Writings by Women on Fat Oppression; Lesbian Love Stories; Finding Courage: Writings by Women* and *The Tribe of Dina: A Jewish Women's Anthology.* I have also been published in a number of feminist and lesbian journals, including *Lesbian Ethics, Sinister Wisdom, Common Lives/Lesbian Lives* and *Broomstick.* My novel, *Keeping it in the Family,* which traces the effects of incest through four generations of one family, is currently in search of a publisher.

ELLEN GRUBER GARVEY: My Jewish background is rooted in relatives and reading, not in formal religious training. It's my mother's relatives, emphatic and bustling with grudges and grievances, who fall more readily into stories. But my father, a whimsical man who changed his name from Cohn to Garvey, probably just to feel out of place when he started writing Jewish children's books, worked for a Jewish organization and brought home the books they published. I can't have been the only ten-year-old reading *Consecrated Unto Me: A Jewish Guide to Love and Marriage* for the good parts. For a long time, in whatever I read, the capital letter *J* used to leap off the page at me: references to *Jews* seemed to be printed in boldface type. Then the word *lesbian* took on that same quality, and for a while I would quickly close such a book, because it was clear to me that if someone saw me reading *That Word* they would make the connection immediately.

I am currently teaching literature and creative writing and working on my doctoral dissertation.

My work has appeared in: *Word of Mouth: Short-Short Stories by Women; The Tribe of Dina: A Jewish Women's Anthology; Feminist Studies; Sinister Wisdom; The Minnesota Review; Paragraph; Sojourner; Shmate* and *Conditions.* A dramatization of "Soup" appears in *Places, Please!: The First Anthology of Lesbian Plays.* I've recently completed a collection of short stories.

SUSAN RUTH GOLDBERG: I was born in New York City and grew up in Inwood, at the Northern tip of Manhattan, an indeterminate neighborhood where the concrete trailed off into the grass and woodland of Inwood Hill Park, and the children of middle-class Jews and working-class Irish hunted for arrowheads in the Indian caves over the Hudson River. As a first-generation American, my Jewish identity received its particular stamp in the left-wing secular Yiddish movement, where cultural, nonreligious, and politically progressive aspects of Jewish life were stressed, along with Yiddish, which was taught both as a folk and as a literary language.

I am a Yiddish folksinger, currently at work on my third recording of Yiddish songs.

I have been writing, and thinking about writing, all my life. I've had a short story published in *Word of Mouth: Short-Short Stories by Women*. "Letter from the Warsaw Ghetto" grew out of an exercise assigned in a writing workshop.

JANO: I grew up in Duncan, Oklahoma, a small town on the Bible Belt. We lit candles every Friday night, weren't allowed to draw or cut on Shabbos, and always drank our milk before eating meat. Meanwhile, my best friends trotted off to church every Wednesday and Sunday night, weren't allowed to dance and never saw my Papa's beer hidden in the back of the icebox. Living in small town Oklahoma made me different because I was a Jew. When I moved to Illinois, Detroit, and New York, I was different because I was a small town Oklahoma Jew. Coming out as a lesbian and a feminist in the early '70s made me different from both my small town and my Jewish friends. And the sexism of my Jewish past made me want to forget my Jewishness altogether. My involvement with a dogmatic leftist group pushed me even further away from my Jewishness and my lesbianism as well. Brittle from all of those experiences of differentness, I began writing to make sense of it all. Now my "dybbuk" character has taken on a life of her own. She mixes Yiddish, lesbianism, and Oklahoma twang. Sometimes she even throws in a smidgen of union organizing. Meanwhile, I live as an artist and union organizer in Oakland with my son, Jonah.

My work has appeared in *Sinister Wisdom, Common Lives/Lesbian Lives, Tradeswomen* and *Jewish Women's Newsletter*.

SUE KATZ: I am an ex-American old gay, living in Israel since 1977, where our Middle Eastern closet is deep, dark and depressing. I am forty-two years old and from a working-class background. What keeps me in Israel is my career: I founded and am head instructor in two Tae Kwon Do (Korean Karate) gyms (the only woman in the profession in the country), and also teach self-defense courses to women, religious girls, and the elderly. I am political, and right now am most active in the anti-Occupation organization "Women in Black."

In the twenty years that I have been writing, I have published journalistic articles, political essays and short stories, most recently in *Common Lives/Lesbian Lives, The Jewish Socialist* and *The Feminist Review.*

MELANIE KAYE/KANTROWITZ: I was born and raised in Brooklyn, graduated from City College of New York, and earned a Ph.D. in Comparative Literature from the University of California, Berkeley. I worked in the Civil Rights Movement in Harlem in the early '60s and have continued as an activist in anti-war, feminist, lesbian and progressive Jewish politics, including Middle East peace work, with Vermont Jewish Women's Call for Peace and New Jewish Agenda. From 1983-87 I edited *Sinister Wisdom,* one of the oldest lesbian/feminist journals, and I am on the Editorial Advisory Board for *Bridges.* I work with the independent study Graduate Program at Vermont College.

A collection of my short fiction, *My Jewish Face and Other Stories,* will be published by Spinsters/Aunt Lute in 1990. I was the co-editor of *The Tribe of Dina: A Jewish Women's Anthology* and I have contributed poetry, fiction, essays and reviews to numerous feminist, lesbian and progressive Jewish journals. My work has appeared in many anthologies, including: *Out the Other Side: A Lesbian Prose Anthology; Naming the Waves: A Lesbian Poetry Anthology; Nice Jewish Girls: A Lesbian Anthology* and *Lesbian Love Stories.*

IRENA KLEPFISZ: I was raised, and remain, a committed secular Jew. I think Jewish secularism and Yiddish culture could be viable alternatives for Jewish identity in the future if we will them to be. I am interested in promoting Yiddish women writers, past and present, through translation. I am an activist in both the lesbian and Jewish communities, and have spent much of the past two years working with the Committee to End the Occupation of the West Bank and Gaza (which I co-founded).

I am the co-editor of *The Tribe of Dina: A Jewish Women's Anthology.* Two companion volumes of my writings, *A Few Words in the Mother Tongue: Poems Selected and New* and *Selected Essays, Speeches and Some Diatribes,* will be published by Eighth Mountain Press in 1990.

HARRIET MALINOWITZ: Regarding being a Jewish lesbian — I'm not sure what to say, aside from the fact that I am one. It wasn't until I was in graduate school, when a friend from Boston referred to "the Jewish intellectual/political tradition," that I started to realize there was one. The very insular Jewish community I grew up in, obsessed with marriage, reproduction, lavish suburban bar mitzvahs and the buying of Israeli bonds, was not a source of pride or inspiration to me, and did not instill any of the values I hold as an adult. I doubt that I will ever smile with familiar affection at words like "matzoh balls," but I do love Jewish food and I gravitate toward eccentric Jewish characters in life as in fiction. To identify as a Jew, and to never consider identifying as a lesbian, were dual dictums thrust upon me in childhood, one of course more explicitly than the other. Now, in my mid-thirties, being a lesbian is more important to me because it has evolved from my own perceived needs and experiences, and keeps me in a constant state of creative dissonance with the world. Being Jewish in New York is too normal and comfortable to do that, but I'm glad to say that discovering "the Jewish intellectual/political tradition" was a distinctly upbeat move. I believe that I'll always write about Jewish lesbians in fiction and in drama because that's who I most intensely understand.

My short stories have been included in the following anthologies: *Nice Jewish Girls: A Lesbian Anthology; Love, Struggle and Change: Stories by Women; Lesbian Love Stories; Word of Mouth: Short-Short Writings by Women* and *The Stories We Hold Secret: Tales of Women's Spiritual Development.* I have had work published in the following journals: *Conditions, Sinister Wisdom, The Massachusetts Review, Chomo Uri,* and *Tat Rama.* My first play, *Minus One,* about lesbian friendship and relationships, was produced in June 1989 at the 13th Street Theatre in New York City. I write lesbian stand-up comedy for Sara Cytron and teach writing in a labor studies college program for adults. Information about *Minus One* can be obtained by contacting Sapatona Productions, 23 Waverly Place, #6-H, New York, New York 10003.

MERRIL MUSHROOM: I am a tall, butch, myopic, politically incorrect Ashkenazi mama. I'm a second-generation American, born of Russian/ Polish ancestry. I grew up in the '40s and came out in the '50s, on Miami Beach. I now live on a rural Tennessee hill farm, with an assortment of horses, dogs, cats, chickens, ducks, turkeys and peafowl; five adopted children; and one radical fairie. I loved my *tanteles*.

My stories have appeared in *Common Lives/Lesbian Lives, Lesbian Love Stories* and *Finding Courage: Writings by Women.* My science fiction novel, *Daughters of Khaton,* is available from Lace Publications, who will soon be publishing a collection of my butch stories from the 1950s.

181

LESLÉA NEWMAN: I was born in 1955, in Brooklyn, New York, the daughter of working-class parents, the granddaughter of poor immigrants from Europe. Being Jewish has always been important to me, except for a few years when I needed to rebel and turn away from it. What brought me back to "my roots" was coming out as a lesbian, which helped me realize that I had been different and "other" all along. It is vital to my well-being to be visible as a lesbian and as a Jew. This takes work, for I am more often than not mistaken for a gentile ("Oh, you're too pretty to be Jewish") and a heterosexual woman ("But you have long hair and wear dresses"). Being a Jew and being a lesbian has taught me how to speak up for myself and be proud of who I am, the importance of community, and the importance of working for social justice. I am happily married to a Puerto Rican woman, and one of the strengths of our relationship is the joy of sharing each other's cultures.

I have published a novel, *Good Enough to Eat,* a collection of short stories, *A Letter to Harvey Milk,* and a volume of poems, *Love Me Like You Mean It.* I've recently edited *Bubbe Meisehs by Shayneh Maidelehs: An Anthology of Poetry by Jewish Granddaughters about our Grandmothers,* and my newest volume of short stories, *Secrets,* is forthcoming from New Victoria Publishers in 1990.

MARTHA SHELLEY: I was born in Brooklyn, of Russian/Polish Jewish background. I joined the Daughters of Bilitis in 1967; helped start Gay Liberation Front in 1969; produced the first lesbian radio show in the U.S. for WBAI-FM from 1972-74; and then moved to California, where I worked with the Women's Press Collective until its demise. I began studying history intensively at that point. Being Jewish and female prepared me to deal with gay oppression. I never had a sense of entitlement. I've always lived with the feeling that storm troopers could bust down the door, and with the knowledge that my only defense is to be a loud, pushy Jew and a blatant queer — not to let them lead me quietly away. And to enjoy each kiss as though it might be the last.

I have published poetry, essays and short stories in numerous journals, including *The Ladder, Ms. Magazine, Amazon Quarterly* and *Common Lives/Lesbian Lives.* My work has been anthologized in *Sisterhood is Powerful; Lesbians Speak Out; The Lavender Herring; Nice Jewish Girls: A Lesbian Anthology; Finding Courage: Writings by Women* and *Word of Mouth: Short-Short Stories by Women.* My two volumes of poetry, *Crossing the DMZ* and *Lovers and Mothers* are available from Sefir Press, 729 55th Street, Oakland, CA 94609.

THYME S. SIEGEL: I was born and raised on a backwoods chicken farm during the '40s and '50s. My family was part of a New Jersey farming community that was characterized by political progressivism, Yiddish language and culture, and very stable nuclear families. I grew up in extreme isolation and mysterious despair, identifying most closely with Rima, the bird-girl (whose tribe had all died), and Alice (the brain-girl) in Wonderland. I had an active but secular Jewish identity that evolved from a completely non-religious background. I ignored the fact that I was Jewish for many years, but I eventually began to research the history of Jewish women and to teach Women's Studies classes on this topic.

I wrote "My Mother Was a Light Housekeeper" ten years ago, based on events of fifteen years ago. "Jealousy," a "true fiction" account of life in the women's community in Eugene, Oregon during the 1970s, was published in *Women's Press* (Eugene, Oregon). In 1989 I wrote a critique of contemporary Jewish feminism called "The Empowerment of Jewish Women" (based on a conference of the same name) in which I explore, among other things, the search for community among Jewish lesbians.

JUDITH STEIN: I am a fat, Jewish lesbian from a working-class background. I grew up in Indiana in the '50s; growing up in a small midwestern city provided an early education in ignorance and anti-Semitism. I owe my Jewish identity to the fierce efforts of my mother, Bernice, who taught me what it means to be a Jew. I find the best of Jewish ethics to be constantly and immediately applicable to the struggles of lesbian life. My favorite image is that of my friends, a group of Jewish dykes, sitting around, stroking our chins and asking, "What does it mean to be a Jew? What does it mean to be a dyke?" I am always aware that I am a survivor, and part of a community that is over 5,000 years old.

I am also a founder of Boston Area Fat Liberation and write and distribute factual articles about the relationship between fat, health and food, and about the oppression of fat women in this society.

I have been a lesbian for almost twenty years; coming out was the second best thing I ever did for myself. (The best thing I ever did for myself was refusing to diet ever again when I was fifteen years old.) I can imagine no life richer and full of more opportunities to grow, learn, and be a mensch than a lesbian life. I am happily involved with another fat, Jewish lesbian.

My work has been published in a variety of lesbian/feminist journals, including *Common Lives/Lesbian Lives,* and I've had stories published in *Hear The Silence: Stories of Myth, Magic and Renewal* and

Lesbian Love Stories. I have written a secular but traditional Pesach haggadah, a feminist retelling of the Purim Megillah, and alternative Chanukah blessings. I am currently working on a series of short stories about two fat lesbians, a fashion model and a clothing designer, who meet, fall in love, and work together for years. These stories allow me to indulge two of my great loves: lesbian romance and fashion.

For information about my work, write Bobbeh Meisehs Press (for materials related to Jewish life and culture) or Boston Area Fat Liberation at P.O. Box 308, Kendall Square, Cambridge, MA 02142.

IRENE ZAHAVA (editor): I was born in the Bronx in 1951 and grew up in a secular household with no formal religious training, but with a strong identity as a cultural Jew. For years, I assumed that the way my family did things was the Jewish way to do them . . . it took a long time to realize that farina, mercurochrome and mylanta were not Yiddish words.

I have been the owner of a feminist bookstore in upstate New York since 1981. I am also an editor for The Crossing Press, working on lesbian and feminist titles and The WomanSleuth Mystery Series. I have edited the following short story anthologies, all published by The Crossing Press: *Hear the Silence; Love, Struggle and Change; Through Other Eyes; Lesbian Love Stories; Finding Courage; Word of Mouth; The WomanSleuth Anthology* and *The Second WomanSleuth Anthology.*